SHEILA LEWIS

THE LEGACY OF THE TOWER

Complete and Unabridged

LINFORD
Leicester

First published in Great Britain in 2008

First Linford Edition
published 2009

British Library CIP Data

Lewis, Sheila
 The legacy of the tower.—Large print ed.—
Linford romance library
 1. Love stories
 2. Large type books
 I. Title
 823.9′2 [F]

 ISBN 978–1–84782–529–2

Published by
F. A. Thorpe (Publishing)
Anstey, Leicestershire

Set by Words & Graphics Ltd.
Anstey, Leicestershire
Printed and bound in Great Britain by
T. J. International Ltd., Padstow, Cornwall

THE LEGACY OF THE TOWER

Lizanne Naismith is saddened when Jeffrey Falkin, owner of her former ancestral home, Gilliestoun Tower, dies in an accident. The grief of his family turns to shock and denial when an unknown son, Alex, turns up. Lizanne is the only one to befriend him, much to the chagrin of her boyfriend Steven, Jeffrey's son. Using her skills as a researcher she investigates Alex's mysterious background. When a long-buried secret is revealed, it alters the lives of everyone involved.

Books by Sheila Lewis
in the Linford Romance Library:

FOR LOVE OF LUCIA
DESTROY NOT THE DREAM
A PROMISE FOR TOMORROW
KENNY, COME HOME
STARS IN HER EYES
A MAN WITH NOWHERE TO GO
LOVE'S SWEET BLOSSOM
AT THE HEART OF THE ISLE
WINGS OF THE DOVES
PETTICOAT PRESS
SHADOW IN RED

1

The peace and tranquility of the sunlit morning matched by my contented mood were shattered when the police car crept up to Gilliestoun Tower. Immediately I left my barn and crossed the drive to meet the two police officers who stepped from the car. I didn't recognise them so they weren't local. Tall, broad men who looked capable of handling anything, but whose expressions presently spoke concern.

'I'm looking for the Falkin family,' the heavier officer said.

'Everyone is away from home this weekend,' I told him. 'I'm Lizanne Naismith, a close family friend. Can I help?'

He identified himself and his fellow officer. 'I'm afraid that there has been an accident,' he said and my thoughts immediately flew to Steven.

'Mr Falkin?' I managed to ask.

To my horror the police officer nodded. 'A road accident in Aberdeenshire.'

'But he's gone to Rotterdam,' I said.

'Mr Jeffrey Falkin?' the officer asked.

'Oh, that's Steven's father,' I explained then took in the significance of the out-of-town officer's presence at the Tower. Whatever had happened called for a visit rather than a telephone call.

'Was it a serious accident?' My voice was shaky.

One look at the sombre expressions told me the worst.

'He's dead?' I whispered.

'I'm afraid so,' the officer said. 'His car left the road on a bad bend in Aberdeenshire and it tumbled into a river.' He turned and looked at the barn where I'd been working when I heard the police car approach.

'Is that your place, Miss Naismith?' he asked.

I nodded.

'Since there's no-one at home here,

2

we'll go back to Drumbroar police station in the meantime. Will you telephone us as soon as the family returns?' he asked. 'We have to speak with them.'

I promised I would. They must have travelled from Aberdeen to see the family specially.

I went back to my barn. As it was Sunday, my museum was closed. I'd been updating my records and dusting the display cases and sweeping the floor. I hadn't planned to stay long as outside the sun was sending beams straight on to the rhododendrons which flanked Gilliestoun Tower.

Today was for the outdoors, for a walk in the hills beyond Drumbroar town. Solitary, yes, because Steven was away on family business.

The barn was unique of its kind, having two rectangular windows set along the wall that faced the tower. They provided light for the museum and also allowed me to keep an eye on Gilliestoun. My Gilliestoun, as I still thought of it.

It was while gazing at the Tower that I had noticed the police car approach. I'd gone to speak to the officers as I knew that Jeffrey Falkin was visiting his sister in Arizona and that Steven was in Rotterdam on business. Evelyn, Jeffrey's wife, had told their daily, Bess Murray, that she was spending the weekend in Edinburgh with friends. The Tower was therefore empty.

Now, work abandoned, I sat in something of a daze, shattered by the news. Jeffrey Falkin at 59 had the energy and bearing of a much younger man. The owner of Falkin Freight, the major company in the small town of Drumbroar, he was a self-made man. He'd dedicated his life to building up his business from one initial lorry to the grand fleet he now commanded and which was expanding into Europe.

An astute business mind coupled with a desire to be respected in the town, he had jumped at the opportunity to buy Gilliestoun Tower when my grandfather had run out of money to fund its upkeep after it had been in the family for generations. The Tower was a traditional fortalice, or fortified manor house, originally built in the seventeenth century.

Jeffrey had cleverly bought up all Grandfather's debts, giving him no option but to sell and move out. Grandfather Lindsay had lost heart when my grandmother, Elizabeth Anne, died and although he later came to live with my parents, he passed away quite soon after.

My mother had retained ownership of the barn in the grounds of the Tower and I had inherited it on her death. I clung on to it with a ferocity that was probably due to my thrawn nature inherited from my earlier forebears.

I saw Jeffrey's wife, Evelyn, arrive home and I telephoned the police station. When the policemen returned I went over to the Tower, thinking that she might need some support on hearing the tragic news.

She had taken the officers up the

spiral staircase to the solar. This was the main room of the Tower, a long rectangular room comfortably furnished with sofas and chairs. I loved it. To my surprise Jeffrey had asked if I would leave the portrait of my grandmother, Elizabeth Anne, on the wall above the fireplace where it had hung for many years. I'd agreed at once, knowing not only was it the right place for the portrait, but it acted as a kind of talisman — for the eventual restoration of my historic right.

Evelyn's face had paled when the officer explained what had happened and she trembled a moment, but otherwise she appeared in control.

'Shall I get some tea?' I offered.

'Yes, and phone Julia,' Evelyn said.

The officers looked concerned that Evelyn sounded so abrupt, but they were not to know it was her usual way of communicating with me. The acquisition of the Tower had given Evelyn the status she always wanted, but she resented my ownership of the barn among other things.

I telephoned her daughter, Julia, at the nearby Dunure farm, not to give her the news, but to summon her to the Tower.

Evelyn and Julia were clearly stamped as mother and daughter. There were elements of beauty in their features, but spoiled by cold eyes and petulant mouths.

Julia was transparently shocked when given the news on her arrival, but she too did not cry. Jeffrey had been something of an autocrat in the family, but I felt he deserved better than this.

The police officers left and Evelyn nodded at me. 'You can go now. It isn't your place to be with us. I will tell Steven about his father when he returns. And close that museum. Show some respect for my husband,' Evelyn said coldly.

All I could think about was Steven. He would be devastated by the loss of his father. And I wanted to be near him to comfort him. Not possible now. Evelyn had seen to that. In fact Evelyn did everything she could to ruin the relationship between us.

I heard voices as soon as I returned to the museum and opened the door.

'There you are!' Christina Dunure's voice boomed across the barn. 'What's the crisis that causes me to drive Julia here?'

'Hi, Lizanne. That's a wicked sword up there,' Julia's son, Rory, pointed at a claymore hung on hooks high on the wall out of reach of eight-year-olds such as him.

'It's a claymore with a really fierce history. I'll tell you some other time,' I told him kindly, then turned to Christina and sent her a warning look, accompanied by a brief shake of my head.

'Hmph,' Christina marched over to my desk and switched on the kettle. Julia's mother-in-law was, like me, a real Drumbroar original. Her family had farmed the area outside town for generations. Christina was all angles, even taller than my five feet eleven inches. She cared not a fig for appearance, presently clad in trousers which had once been half of her late husband's Sunday suit, topped with a sweatshirt, embroidered with gambolling lambs, half of whose ears were missing.

Her passion was her pigs, who she always named on wooden plaques nailed above the sties and she even had Chopin piped in to comfort them. I knew she played the piano to concert standard, but had always refused to consider a career in music. I was very fond of her.

'Jeffrey has had a car accident,' I now spoke too quietly for Rory to overhear.

'And?' Christina, as ever, was direct.

I shook my head.

Christina pursed her lips. 'Poor guy. I'll miss his vitality.'

For a moment I was surprised at her comment. Perhaps Christina saw more than everyone suspected. I too would miss Jeffrey's vitality. I bore him no personal grudge for taking over my inheritance. He was the one who seemed uneasy about it, always being rather distant with me.

I persuaded Christina to take Rory over to the Tower as I wanted to leave. Fetching my bike from a cubby-hole at the back of the barn, I locked up and cycled down the hill to Drumbroar. My home was a flat over what I called 'Dad's shop'.

The building was in fact late Georgian and one of the finest pieces of architecture in Drumbroar. The ground floor had been converted to offices for the legal firm of Clark and Naismith.

My father, Hamish Naismith, had bought the top floor of the house when we decided to move from our villa some time after mother died ten years earlier. Now we had twin flats, one for him and the other for me.

I tried to keep my thoughts occupied by preparing a light lunch and waited for him to return from the golf course.

'You're home early,' he commented

when I opened my door to him and asked him in.

'Slacking again?' he teased as I didn't immediately answer him.

He really didn't understand what had made me give up an opportunity to take up a good offer of research work with my old university. Instead I used my history degree to investigate and record all the artefacts I collected from all over Scotland for the museum.

As a sideline I undertook family research for anyone interested, whether it was missing relatives, lost family paintings or other heirlooms. I diligently searched old parish records for ancestors and even undertook research for busy authors. Those earnings kept me fed and my bicycle in good condition.

I gave him a dram then told him the sad news. The glass was halted halfway to his lips and he slowly put it down on the table.

'It doesn't seem right,' was his first comment and I understood right away what he meant. 'He can't be dead. Not Jeffrey. He was always so . . . so alive!'

I noticed a fleeting range of expressions cross his face, some of which I couldn't put a finger on. The two men had not been particularly close, but it had been something of a shock when Jeffrey had chosen the younger Peter Clark to handle his legal business rather than Dad when his original solicitor had retired ten years ago.

I was too young at the time to pay much attention, but in the ensuing years I'd noticed that Jeffrey had kept Dad at a distance, refusing invitations to golf matches and other functions. That had nothing at all to do with Gilliestoun, as in my case, but I didn't understand it.

I noticed then that Dad was genuinely upset and we just picked at the meal, talking over the various events that had marked Jeffrey's life.

'Does Steven know?' Dad said eventually.

I looked at my watch. 'I don't know

when he was due home from Rotterdam, but I was sent packing in case he
arrived while I was still there.'

'Surely Evelyn is not going to keep
up this farce of pretending you don't
mean a lot to each other?'

'Probably more so now,' I shrugged.

'Why?'

'Presumably as the eldest, Steven will
inherit Gilliestoun,' I pointed out.
Although genuinely grieving for Jeffrey's death, that thought had risen
unbidden to my mind while waiting for
Dad.

'Ah, and when you marry, you'll be
back in your old home and she'll be
out,' Hamish gave me an old-fashioned
look.

'In the first place, Steven and I
haven't ever discussed marriage,' I
replied a trifle testily. 'And I would
never throw Evelyn out of her home.'

Hamish leant over and took my
hand. 'Sorry, my dear, that was
extremely offensive of me. It's just . . . '

'What?'

'I want to be certain that you are clear-eyed about Steven.'

'So do I,' I was honest with him. I loved Steven and had done so since we were children.

My heart went out to him when he arrived at the flat late that evening. He looked bewildered and confused. I slipped my arms round his waist and he laid his head on my shoulder. I just held him for several minutes, murmuring condolences and sympathy.

He was taller than Jeffrey by several inches and did not have the strong facial features of his father. It could be said that he was conventionally handsome with his raven hair and deep blue eyes.

'Come on, sit down. You've had a terrible shock.' I led him to the sofa.

'More than one,' he said very quietly.

I stared at him.

It took him a moment or two to settle himself.

'There was something funny going on in Rotterdam with Broq,' he began.

14

'I thought you were there to sort out a new haulage contract with that company.'

'So did I, but the directors there knew something about Falkin Freight that I didn't,' he had been gazing down at his linked hands, but now he raised his head and looked at me directly.

'But you are your dad's second in command,' I floundered a little. It was no secret that Jeffrey had rarely, if ever, really delegated anything to Steven.

'Once they realised I didn't know what deal had been agreed, they clammed up. I caught the first plane home to ask Dad what he was up to,' he shrugged. 'It was only when it came in to land that I remembered he'd gone to visit Aunt Sarah in Arizona.'

I stared at him and he stared back. I asked the question that had been puzzling me and one that no-one else had posed.

'So how come he had an accident in Aberdeenshire?'

'Exactly,' Steven nodded.

'Wasn't your dad meant to be the one going to see Broq?' I asked.

'Oh yes, but then he told me that Aunt Sarah had called asking him to visit and so he decided to send me to Rotterdam instead. No other reason.' He couldn't keep a trace of bitterness from his tone.

Then he shook his head. 'I feel I'm betraying him. He's dead and all I can think of is what he was hiding.'

'It's not a bad thing at the moment,' I gently reassured him. 'In a way it will help you cope with the shock. One minute you're coping and the next it hits you like a sledgehammer. And it isn't over quickly.'

'Your mother?' he asked quietly.

I nodded. 'I still have some dark days,' I didn't elaborate on those.

'Help me through this, Lizanne,' he said after a moment.

I just held him and he knew I would.

After he'd gone I tried to think about the relationship Steven had had with his father. They weren't particular friends, I knew that. Jeffrey had insisted that Steven follow him into the family business. It wasn't what Steven wanted at all. His ambition was to be his own boss and his passion lay with speed and sport — the more extreme the better. He wanted to be involved in anything dangerous and glamorous, not play second fiddle to his father and move haulage lorries around. I wondered what the future held for him now and with Falkin Freight.

Next morning I surfaced with the sound of the telephone ringing. It was Evelyn.

'I need you here to help with the funeral arrangements,' she said. 'We have to inform all Jeffrey's business contacts. Our depot manager is out of the country at the moment and I don't want to rely on his office staff.'

It took me a few moments to realise that what she wanted was not me, but the use of my computer — with me as operator.

Well, it was the least I could do in the

circumstances I thought as I cycled back to Gilliestoun. The Tower is set on a hill about a mile west of Drumbroar which is not large enough to qualify as a major town, but has long ago overspilled its original village classification.

It is neatly divided in two by Loch Broar, which is fed by streams from Ben Broar, a protective mountain sentinel to the north. There is a good community spirit in the town and its main employer is Falkin Freight. I knew Jeffrey's office staff were more than competent, but I guessed Evelyn wanted to have personal control over the funeral arrangements.

When I arrived I rapped on the heavy oak front door of the Tower. It was promptly opened by Bess Murray. She was a local woman, with a husband and three children at home. She was a fine example of a typical Scot, hardworking with a devastatingly pithy tongue. I reckoned, however, she had her work cut out with Evelyn.

This morning she looked pale and drawn. I knew she'd liked Jeffrey and guessed she was genuinely mourning his passing.

'Hi, Lizanne,' she gave me a peck on the cheek. We were good friends.

'They're upstairs in the solar,' she indicated with her head. 'I'm bringing up coffee and biscuits in a sec.'

As was her custom, Evelyn was sitting with her back to my grandmother's portrait. Steven was by one of the windows and sent me a coded loving look. We never paraded our relationship in front of Evelyn.

Julia sat on one of the sofas and her husband, Todd, lounged in an armchair. It was difficult for me to believe that Christina could have given birth to Todd. He had none of her fire or generosity of spirit. Today he was wearing a tweed suit of a colour and texture that reminded me of orange peel. He always tried to appear as landed gentry but never quite got it right. There was an ever-present smile, close to a smirk on his face, that set my teeth on edge. Some facet of his personality must have attracted Julia, but I had a suspicion that the marriage had gone sour in recent years.

Evelyn handed me a list of people to e-mail.

'Advise everyone of our loss and then in a day or two you can send them details of the funeral,' she said.

'Why not wait until we've made the arrangements, Mother?' Steven suggested.

'I don't want his business associates hearing the news from the press,' she said. 'He was much too an important figure for that.'

At that moment Bess brought in the coffee, just as I was on the point of being dismissed.

'I take it you can't arrange the funeral until you know when Jeffrey's sister will arrive?' I asked.

Silence fell.

'You did telephone Aunt Sarah?' Steven asked his mother.

'I thought you would do that for me,' Evelyn didn't look at Steven as she helped herself to coffee.

'Actually I'm surprised she hasn't been on the phone to us,' Steven said. 'She must be wondering why Dad didn't arrive in Arizona.'

Evelyn put her cup down. 'I don't know exactly when she was expecting him. You know how he always liked to be flexible with arrangements.'

'I'm just wondering why he left us, saying he was going to Glasgow Airport to catch a flight to the States and then he drove to Aberdeen,' Steven tried to sound casual.

'Something must have come up in connection with the business,' Julia said. 'Dad always put that first.'

'Don't you know what it was all about, Steven? I thought you were Jeffrey's right hand man,' Todd said in a careless tone, designed to conceal the jibe.

'Since I'd gone to Rotterdam I was hardly in a position to know about

21

last-minute arrangements,' Steven allowed himself to be nettled.

Steven consulted his watch. 'It's too early to phone Aunt Sarah on account of the time difference. I'll do it this afternoon.'

To our surprise, Bess appeared in the solar again.

'There's a gentleman downstairs asking to see you,' she announced, not looking at anyone in particular.

'Who is it?' Evelyn asked.

'He . . . er . . . just said his name was Alex,' Bess was politely vague.

'Someone offering condolences, I expect,' Julia said.

'Shall I show him up?' Bess asked.

'I'm just leaving for the office,' Steven said. 'I'll see this person downstairs. It's probably business anyway.'

'We must go too, Mother,' Julia jumped up. 'Todd and I have an appointment in town.'

We all trooped downstairs, Bess leading the way — right outside to the driveway.

The man waiting was as tall as Steven, but entirely different in appearance. Dark hair, slightly streaked by the sun topped a strong face which had an odd set to the jaw, as if it had been broken at one time and badly set. His eyes were clear blue. He was wearing a formal suit which looked at odds with his rather loose-limbed frame.

'Good morning,' he began and we all registered the American accent. 'This is a very sad time for all of us and I share your grief.'

There was something odd about this little speech and no-one said anything for a moment.

'I don't think we've met before,' Steven stepped forward and offered his hand to the newcomer. 'I'm Steven Falkin.'

He was rewarded with a crooked smile. 'No, it's been a long time in coming. I'm Alex.'

The stranger then turned to Evelyn and gave her a neat bow. 'Mrs Falkin.' He transferred his glance to Julia.

'Julia,' another nod and he turned to her husband. 'And you must be Todd.'

The man flashed a glance at me, but clearly did not know who I was.

'I'm sorry, but you have the advantage of us,' Steven said. 'We don't know who you are. An associate of Father's?'

The man's body tensed.

'Jeffrey hadn't told you that I was coming to Gilliestoun?' he asked.

'No,' Steven shook his head and glanced at his mother and sister.

'We don't even know your name, young man,' Evelyn said a trifle frostily.

'It's Falkin. Alex Falkin.'

His words seemed to hang suspended in the still morning air and were met by the same silence.

He spoke again. 'I'm Jeffrey's son.'

2

Alex Falkin wandered round the museum looking at my collection but not, I guessed, really seeing them. How could anything register with him? First the loss of his father and then the rejection by the Falkins.

They had left him standing at the front door of Gilliestoun. Evelyn had swept back inside, Steven had driven off and Julia and Todd had followed in their car. I wondered what kind of appointment they had in town that was so urgent that they could not stay and keep Evelyn company.

I had been left outside with Alex Falkin.

'Do you have transport?' I asked him.

'Hired car. It's outside on the road. I need to find somewhere to stay,' he said tonelessly.

'That's my place over there,' I said

pointing to the barn. 'If you like I'll telephone the local hotels, see what accommodation they have. You can park your car behind the barn.'

He gave me a long, searching look. 'Thanks.'

'I'm Lizanne Naismith,' I told him. 'Not family.'

He just nodded at that and walked away to fetch his car. While he did so, I thought over that scene on the front step of Gilliestoun.

Evelyn had been the first to react to Alex's claim that he was Jeffrey's son. 'That's monstrous. I have never heard such an outrageous claim. My husband has just been taken from us and you have the insensitivity to . . . '

'Mother, don't upset yourself.' Steven had taken her arm and then turned to Alex. 'If my father had another son he would have told us,' he said, but I could hear the uncertainty in his voice. It was only yesterday that he'd said Jeffrey had been virtually secretive over other matters.

'Why have we not seen you before?' Julia then asked.

'I was brought up in the States,' Alex said.

I immediately thought of Jeffrey's sister, Sarah, in Arizona and wondered if there was any connection. I said nothing, however, this was a family matter.

'I was adopted,' Alex Falkin went on. 'I didn't know that Jeffrey was my father until I was twelve years of age. He always promised I could come to Scotland. Now I'm here,' his voice faded a little. 'Too late.'

'Have you any proof?' Evelyn sounded waspish and I suddenly felt sorry for her. It looked like Jeffrey had betrayed her and that must have been a terrible shock.

Alex Falkin looked at her, his expression a mixture of distress and something approaching understanding. 'I didn't expect I'd need proof, but after what has happened,' he paused. 'I guess I am something of a shock.'

'The thing is, we know nothing about you,' Steven began. 'Your claim seems . . . well, incredible. I think we should leave it for the meantime. Perhaps if you come back tomorrow . . . '

'Steven! I will not have this man in my home,' Evelyn interrupted.

Alex Falkin took a step back, but he didn't walk away. 'Fine,' he said tersely. 'Next time we meet, I'll have proof of my identity.' it was clear he intended that there would be a next time whether at Evelyn's home or elsewhere.

* * *

'How come you have a museum in the grounds of Gilliestoun?' Alex now asked me.

'The Tower is my old ancestral home. Jeffrey bought it from my grandfather, but my mother retained ownership of the barn. I decided to open it as a museum when I inherited it.'

'Ancestral home? Does that mean that Gilliestoun was in your family for years?' he looked mystified.

'Centuries, actually. You need to know a lot about Scottish history to appreciate the old clan system and how strongholds were established and maintained through the generations,' I told him.

'It must have been tough to lose it.'

'It was, although I have to say that your dad took good care of the Tower,' I said and meant it.

His eyes took on a sharp look. 'My dad? Then you believe that I'm his son?'

I shrugged. 'I guess you will have to provide proof, but you walk just like him.' I had noticed the similar rolling gait as he'd walked away to fetch his car.

Alex Falkin raised his eyebrows. 'You'd make a good photographer with your keen eyes, Miss Naismith,' he said.

'Just call me Lizanne,' I answered. 'Anyway, as an historian I've been trained to be observant. Part of the job.'

While he'd been walking around the museum, I'd made some instant coffee.

'Here, have this. Not what you're used to in the States I reckon, but it's hot and warm,' I handed him a mug.

He attempted a smile. 'I drink most things without complaint. I've lived rough from time to time.'

I looked at his jaw and he noticed. 'Yeah, I've been in a few fights and it shows, doesn't it?' he was as sharp as the point of one of my swords.

I avoided commenting on that. 'I'll fix a hotel for you. How long do you want to stay?' I asked.

'I intend to be at Dad's funeral, then . . . ' he stopped. 'I planned to stay for some time originally, see something of the country, find out about my Dad's heritage.'

The word *heritage* stopped me in my tracks. If he truly was Jeffrey's son would he stand to inherit something . . . like a third of Gilliestoun?

He downed the coffee in one go. 'To be honest it's been a brutal shock finding out that Dad didn't tell any of the family about me. I know all about them, what they look like, what they do, how the rooms are furnished in the Tower. He even told me who he played golf with, the details of the freight business,' he looked at me. 'He never mentioned you.'

I shrugged. 'No need to.'

Involuntarily Alex's eyes flickered around the museum. I guessed he thought he should have been told about it and me. I couldn't enlighten him. Jeffrey always kept me at arms' length. I never knew why.

'You know, although no-one has heard of you, it could be because Jeffrey didn't want to hurt Evelyn with the news of another son,' I said.

'I don't see why. It can't affect her or their marriage in any way. I was born before he met her,' he said.

'Were you born in the States?' I asked, thinking maybe Jeffrey had had a relationship over there.

'Sure was. This is my first visit to Scotland. Dad always said it would be difficult to bring me here. I could never see why,' I could detect the bitterness in his tone.

Difficult? I would have said awkward, embarrassing, volatile — all possible. Alex had been told about Jeffrey's family, but clearly not how they thought or behaved. I suspected he'd stepped into a minefield. Jeffrey must have known that would have been his family's reaction.

'What did your mother think?' I said tentatively.

'I never knew her,' he replied tightly. 'She's dead now I've been told.'

'I'm sorry,' I apologised at once. 'That was an intrusive question.'

He gave me a wry smile. 'No, I guess you're trying to help. Some far out cousins of Dad's adopted me and I had a great childhood. Dad visited about twice a year as *Uncle Jeffrey*. When I got to about twelve I realised someone was paying for school fees and lots of extras I knew my adoptive parents couldn't afford.'

'So he told you exactly who he was,' I said.

Alex laughed harshly at the memory. 'I threw it at him, told him I'd guessed. He broke down, said he would have told me in time.'

'But he didn't say he'd bring you here,' I asked.

'No, not right away. I was full of resentment — oh not about Scotland then, just that I felt I'd been deceived and I gave him a rough time,' he shrugged.

'So why now?' I asked softly.

'After all these years?' He sighed. 'I haven't been the ideal son. Flunked college, drifted from job to job over the years. Became something of a bum as we call it in the States. I began to wonder if I might make something of my life in Scotland. I wanted Dad to be proud of me — show me off to his family. He was due to visit me, but I jumped the gun and told him I was coming to Scotland.'

'And he agreed?' I asked, remembering Jeffrey had told everyone he was visiting Arizona.

'I thought so when I told him I

wanted to try somewhere new,' Alex paused. 'He told me to fly into Aberdeen airport,' he got up and wandered restlessly round the barn again. 'Now I know he hadn't told the family here so maybe he planned to meet me and put me right back on a flight to the States.'

I had no answer to that. It seemed very probable, although now we'd never know what Jeffrey had planned.

I picked up the phone, called the Drumbroar Arms and reserved a room for three nights. I gave the name *Falkin* and guessed the receptionist would assume it was just a relative of the family. No need for her, or anyone else here, to know at the moment just how close a relative of the family.

'How do I get there?'

'If you give me a lift into town in your car, I'll direct you,' I said.

We arrived at the hotel and before I got out of the car, he said: 'By the way, on the matter of identification. Someone here in Drumbroar must know about me.'

'How do you know that?' I was stunned. No-one here had ever even hinted that Jeffrey had another son.

'I discovered that my school and college fees were paid through a trust, not directly by Dad. I guess he must have a lawyer in town?'

'Yes, Peter Clark. His offices are in the town square. You can't miss them. I have a flat on the top floor of the building,' I told him.

'Right,' he said crisply, got out of the car and walked into the hotel without another word.

Feeling dismissed I marched away, but before long my sympathy for him resurfaced. The loss of his father, rejection by the family and left alone to mourn. Could I do anything? Like have him for a meal? But I rejected that. It wasn't my place.

Besides, there was a whole parcel of questions in my mind, such as where in the States did he hail from? Did he know Jeffrey's sister, Sarah? True to my investigative nature, I wanted the answers, but this wasn't my family business and it would have been insensitive at least to have hounded Alex. I would have to find out by other means.

I made my way home with the intention of talking to Dad as soon as possible. I wondered if he knew about Alex and had kept quiet all those years. After all, he was Peter Clark's partner in the legal business.

I went straight to his flat and gave him a resume of the day's events.

'A son hidden away in the States for thirty years?' was his first reaction, accompanied by a short bark of laughter. 'Do me a favour, Lizzie, that's straight out of the joke book!'

'I think he could be telling the truth,' I said soberly.

He regarded me with some scepticism and then said: 'Let's examine what facts we have.'

I sat down, too weary to protest against the precise legal approach, devoid of emotion. I'd never have made a lawyer.

'Jeffrey is the father. Who is the mother?'

I shrugged. 'Alex doesn't know and she's dead.'

'Convenient.'

'What's that supposed to mean?' I asked.

'The only two people who definitely know he is a Falkin are dead,' he pointed out.

'His adoptive parents must know,' I made a mild protest.

'That might not be actual proof either as far as the law is concerned,' Dad said.

'Alex thinks there must be some details of the trust Jeffrey set up, probably lodged with Peter Clark,' I said.

Dad was silent for a moment. 'If there are, it's news to me. Then again, if definite proof is needed there is always DNA to make certain.'

I sank deeper into the armchair.

There seemed to be something very cold about testing. Like a last resort and somehow I felt that would upset Alex more.

'Did this Alex Falkin say if his parents were married?' Dad asked.

'No. I just assumed they weren't. Had they been, there would be no reason for Jeffrey to have Alex adopted, would there?'

'And no reason for him to keep his son in the States while he had another family here,' Dad paused. 'It sounds fishy to me.'

'In what way?'

'It all feels a bit convenient, like arriving when he did when Jeffrey is no longer around. Almost like someone smelling an inheritance and making a false claim,' Dad said.

'Alex hardly knew Jeffrey was going to die in an accident,' I challenged.

'Yes, there is that. Sorry, love, just my legal mind trying to spot impostors, it happens so often,' he spread his hands in half apology.

'Anyway, he says he's coming to see Peter Clark tomorrow. Make sure you find out what happens,' I told him.

Since I had left my bike at the museum in order to accompany Alex in his car, I had to borrow Dad's car to get to Gilliestoun next morning.

I wasn't surprised to see Steven stride across from the Tower as soon as I put my key in the museum door. His face was like thunder.

I tried to head him off at the pass, as it were.

'Hi, love, I half expected a phone call from you last night.' I gave him a tender smile as he followed me into the museum.

'Oh, would there have been any answer? Weren't you still at the Drumbroar Arms with the yank calling himself Falkin?' his voice was tight with anger.

I knew Steven very well and although surprised at the sarcasm wondered if he was angry that I had spent time with Alex Falkin. But that was hardly my fault as the whole family had initially rejected him.

'Your information was not very accurate,' I said pretending not to notice his tone and switching on my computer. 'I only directed Alex Falkin to the hotel, left him outside and had to walk home.'

'Why is he staying there anyway?'

'Steven, he intends to stay for the funeral,' I said as gently as possible, omitting Alex's comment about staying in the area for a while.

'The funeral! He can't come to that! It would kill Mother.' He flung himself into the chair opposite my desk.

'Your mother has not been betrayed, Steven. Alex was born before Jeffrey met your mother.'

'Did he tell you that? Have you swallowed whole everything he said?' he demanded.

'He reckons your dad's lawyer has proof of his birth.'

'So that's what it's about,' Steven thumped a fist into the palm of the other hand. 'Peter Clark phoned earlier. He's coming to Gilliestoun this morning to discuss business with us,' he said.

I stared at him. 'You mean, like the will?'

Steven shrugged. 'It isn't the reading of the will. He said he'd had a phone call from that person calling himself Alex Falkin.'

'So it's true then,' I almost whispered the words.

'Oh, Lizanne, how do I know?' he cried. 'If it's true how could my father have done this to us? Sprung a brother on us?'

I immediately went round the desk and slipped my arms about him. He was terribly distressed, but more, it seemed, from his father's behaviour than the existence of Alex.

'He might have been shielding you from hurt,' I said, only I didn't think that was Jeffrey's style, but Steven desperately needed comforting. 'One day he would have told you,' I went on placatingly. 'Don't forget, your father expected to be around for some time.'

'It's been thirty years according to what you were told. He was taking his time to tell us,' he said bitterly.

'Don't blame your father until you know the real facts,' I said, then attempted to shift the emphasis. 'Have you told your Aunt Sarah about your dad?'

'Yes, I rang her last night. She was completely shocked and distressed.'

'She would be doubly so if she was expecting Jeffrey to visit her,' I said, knowing it was a leading statement. If she'd been expecting Jeffrey then he had been going to see her and not Alex.

Steven shrugged. 'I forgot about that and she didn't mention it.'

I said nothing, but it looked to me like confirmation that Jeffrey had been lying about visiting her and really planned to see Alex instead. That would be some way to validating Alex's claim.

'Aunt Sarah is flying in the day after tomorrow for the funeral. Will you come with me to the airport to meet her?' he asked.

'Of course, my love,' I kissed him gently on his cheek. I would give him all the support he needed.

'Now, have you a list of all the people I have to notify?' I asked. It was definitely time to move on, give Steven something positive to do.

He sat beside me as I set up the computer and together we composed a letter to all the people Evelyn had listed. While I set up the printer he returned to the Tower.

I heard the door open again about half an hour later and assumed he'd returned, but my hackles rose when I heard the oily tones of Todd Dunure's voice behind me.

'What a sensation,' he drawled. 'Unknown spawn of the old man.'

'Oh, for goodness sake, Todd, stop speaking like an old B movie actor,' I didn't even bother to turn round.

He slid into the chair recently vacated by Steven. 'You must be feeling rather nervous,' he went on.

At that I swung round in my chair to

face him. 'What do you mean?'

'Gilliestoun. Re-possession might not be on the cards after all,' he said slyly.

I didn't pretend with Todd. Much as I disliked him I couldn't deny that we sprang from the same tradition — land and property. He took it as natural that I should want to possess Gilliestoun again. He probably also thought that I had decided on marriage to Steven for that very purpose.

I remembered that his father had wanted to buy Gilliestoun himself when Grandfather had been forced to give it up, but Jeffrey had offered more money.

Maybe Todd's marriage to Julia was an attempt to gain something of the Tower and its lands. I understood that while not necessarily approving of it. I didn't really care what Todd thought about me and Steven. As long as Steven knew that I really loved him.

At the sound of a car arriving we both moved to the barn window. It was Alex's white Fiesta.

'Now this should be interesting,'

Todd said silkily.

I felt my pulse rate quicken. I was uneasy. I didn't think Alex was going to get a good reception and that worried me. I followed Todd to the door of the barn and stood there while he crossed the drive.

Alex was barely out of the car when Steven emerged from the Tower.

'The meeting has been changed to Mr Clark's office in town,' he said coldly and turned away. I noticed Alex watching him with an unreadable expression. Steven helped Evelyn and Julia into his car.

Todd hurried across to join the family, pausing only to throw a comment at Alex.

'Sorry, old chap, it seems you're not allowed to set foot in the old homestead,' his smile was totally false.

Alex spared him with a withering glance. 'Yet,' was all he said.

3

With Bess Murray standing by my side I watched the cars speed off from the Tower. 'I reckon we could do with a cup of coffee,' she said.

I guessed she wanted a chat but I also craved a cup of her coffee, so superior to my own brew in the barn.

'I'll be with you in a minute, I just have to collect some things,' I told her.

I gathered all the funeral notification letters I'd printed, locked the barn and went into Gilliestoun.

The Tower was four storeys high and a solid square shape. The front door led straight into the barrelled-ceiling kitchen with its barred windows. The first floor was dominated by the solar with its long windows overlooking the front and rear. There was also a smaller room used for dining.

Bess had the coffee waiting for me

when I entered the kitchen together with a stack of her melt-in-the-mouth scones.

'What do you think of all this, Lizanne?' she asked and I could hear the sadness in her voice. 'When the American came to the door yesterday, I had a funny feeling about him, but it wasn't until he'd gone that I thought he had a look of Mr Falkin,' she said. 'The same shape of head.'

I hadn't noticed that but she was right.

'Does the family think he's an impostor?' she asked.

'I think they're really confused and upset, this coming at the same time as Mr Falkin's death. But Alex Falkin seems to think that someone here in Drumbroar must at least know of his existence.'

'Is that why they've all gone to see the lawyer?' Bess asked.

'Presumably,' I gave a slight shrug.

Bess gave me a long look and pushed more scones in my direction. 'If he is who he says he is, he'll stand to inherit,' she commented, concern and sympathy in her tone.

I knew at once what she meant. Bess's mother had been housekeeper in the Tower in my grandfather's time and loyalty was embedded in the family still. Many of the Drumbroar folk, I knew, still thought Gilliestoun belonged to me, morally if not legally. It was nothing to do with not liking the Falkins, everything to do with tradition.

'I know, Bess, but I'll still be around to keep an eye on it,' I attacked a scone, more to put an end to talk, although I enjoyed the melting sensation her baking gave me.

When I'd finished I rose from the table. 'Think I'll just go and have a nostalgic browse.'

She nodded understanding. I often did this when the family was not present in the Tower.

I had been in the solar only the day before so I didn't linger there, just long enough to gaze yet again at the portrait of my grandmother, Elizabeth Anne.

Why had nature decreed that I should not inherit her beauty, or the delicate colouring, the neat, feminine frame? Which gene had produced my generous (to put it kindly) build, long limbs, raw-boned look, strong features and plentiful auburn hair? All that beauty in the family and I didn't even rate fine eyebrows? My mother, Anne, on the other hand, had been almost a carbon copy of Grandmother.

The portrait was also a painful reminder of the vacuum left by Mother when she died ten years ago.

When I returned downstairs, Bess was holding the telephone in her hand. She thrust it towards me.

'It's Mr Falkin's sister in America,' she whispered. 'Can you talk to her?'

I took the phone. 'Hello, this is Lizanne,' I said.

There was a silence for a moment then I heard Sarah's voice. 'Lizanne? What are you doing in the Tower?'

I was taken by surprise, yet her tone

wasn't critical, more unsure, I thought. Perhaps she considered that I had no business in the Falkin home.

'Everyone's gone to see the lawyer in town,' I told her. 'I'm just delivering the funeral notification letters I printed.'

'Why have they gone to see the lawyer?' she said sharply. 'He doesn't have the will.'

That took me by surprise again, but I had to say something. It wasn't my place to tell her about Alex, so I just put on a vague tone.

'I don't know, no-one explained.'

'Mmm, I presume the funeral is next week sometime,' Sarah said.

'No, it's this Friday,' I told her.

'But it can't be. There might not be time to ... ' she stopped suddenly. 'Remind Steven to meet me at the airport,' she said and cut the connection as I was about to say: 'I'll see you then.'

Time for what, I asked myself. Why should Sarah need time?

'Something else up?' Bess was gazing

at me with wide eyes.

'Well, it was certainly an odd conversation,' and I repeated the gist of it.

'How does she know that Mr Falkin's lawyer doesn't have his will?' she asked.

'That struck me as odd, too, plus the fact that she apparently needs more time,' I hesitated, wondering if I should be repeating Sarah's words to Bess. It felt like gossip, yet I knew Bess could be trusted implicitly.

However, I judged it time to leave and thanked her for the coffee and scones. I returned to the barn, but for the first time my museum did not comfort me. I wanted to be away from all this — the disruption the family was experiencing, the loss of Jeffrey, which I felt even though he'd never paid me much attention, and my ever present longing for the Tower.

After an hour, I locked the barn and left. I had come in Dad's car but instead of taking the turn for town, I headed off instead for Ben Broar. The sky was overcast and gloomy, just like my mood.

I kept walking gear in the barn and had thrown it into the boot before leaving. There were some good paths on the Ben and I reckoned I needed some strong air to banish the confusion in my mind.

There were a number of cars parked just off the road. One I had not expected to see was Alex's. He was leaning on the bonnet, making some adjustments to a camera.

Swithering whether to speak to him or just take a path out of his line of vision, I left it too late as he turned and saw me.

I noticed his face was closed. He nodded at me.

'Didn't expect to see you here,' I said.

'I'm at a loose end.' I nodded and turned away. I didn't especially want company and he looked as if he'd had enough for the day.

'Before you go,' he called and I

halted. 'Could you point me in the direction of the best viewpoints?'

There was only one major path at this point and others branched off further up the mountain. 'You'll have to follow me for a bit,' I told him.

We trudged up the hill for a while then he said: 'You haven't asked me how the meeting went.'

'I didn't want to pry,' I said.

'Peter Clark produced some legal document signed by Dad saying that Alexander James Falkin was his son and there was a copy of my birth certificate attached to it. He also had details of the trust set up to pay my school fees, etc. That had been arranged by his predecessor in the firm.'

'So it's all legal now,' I said.

'Nope.'

I turned round to face him. 'What do you mean?'

'The family is not convinced that I am Alexander James Falkin. I could be an impostor. The only person who could identify me is my father. And it is too late for that,' Alex said flatly.

'But . . . ' I began.

'I know. DNA testing. I won't have that, Lizanne,' his voice rose. 'I shouldn't have to go through that. I'm determined to find other proof. Did Dad have photographs of me? I have a stack of ones I took of us both, but they're back in the States.'

'Where in the States?' I asked.

'In Tucson, where I grew up. Why do you want to know?'

'Jeffrey's sister lives in Arizona, too. Phoenix to be precise. She's coming over for his funeral. Have you ever met her?' I asked.

'No, he told me about her, but we've never met. Dad never took me to Phoenix. I've no idea if he ever told her about me.'

In a few moments we cleared the tree line. 'Hey, is that Gilliestoun down there?' He pointed at the Tower.

'Yes, pretty impressive, isn't it? That's Loch Broar which became part of the defensive system of the Tower, a necessity during the feuds of old. Nobody could get near Gilliestoun without being spotted by a good lookout.'

'I bet you know every nook and cranny in that place,' he said.

'Sure do.'

He took a couple of photographs. 'I suppose that's what Evelyn and her brood want to keep out of my hands,' he said grimly. 'As if I cared about an inheritance. It was my father I cared about. His family is a cold blooded lot, Lizanne.'

'Alex, it's been a double shock for them,' I tried to explain. 'It can't be you they're against. It has to be Jeffrey for keeping them in the dark all those years. Plus there is all the uncertainty about the future. Jeffrey was such a strong figure, not only in the family but also the town. He controlled everything,' I paused.

Alex put his camera down on the ground with great care. 'What I don't understand is what was Dad waiting for? When was going to be the right moment to tell them?'

'I have to admit that struck me as odd too. The longer he left it, the more difficult it was going to be,' I conceded.

'When I called him and he agreed to meet me in Aberdeen I thought he would have briefed the family by then. Clearly not,' he sighed. 'Perhaps he was just going to bring me here, after his meeting, and surprise them.'

I felt a quiver of interest. 'He had a meeting in Aberdeen?' I was sure Steven knew nothing about that.

'He told me he had to see a business acquaintance before picking me up at the airport,' he said.

'How did the police know where to find you?' I asked as we walked on. The air was distinctly chilly now and mist was beginning to snake round the upper reaches of the Ben.

'There was a note on Dad's car dashboard with my name and the hotel's address. They called on me there. I'd just arrived. I took a cab from the airport when Dad didn't turn up to meet me.'

'Do you still have the note?' I asked.

He swung round to stare at me. 'It would be a form of proof,' I told him.

He shook his head. 'I guess the police must have it. I didn't see it.'

Which was a pity, I thought. It could have been useful to him, if it existed. With a sneaky feeling of horror I realised I too wasn't absolutely sure that he was Alexander James Falkin.

'Say, your dad, Hamish, is a real nice guy,' he said after a moment. 'Met me at the office, rustled up some good coffee and told me he'd miss Dad. Known him for twenty odd years, he said.'

'Yes, Mother and Dad were around the same ages as Jeffrey and Evelyn,' I let it ride at that. They had never been friends. I guessed it all had to do with the sale of Gilliestoun.

'I was surprised that he wasn't Dad's lawyer. Peter Clark is much younger,' Alex said.

I shrugged. 'Jeffrey transferred his business to Peter when the senior lawyer retired.' I didn't add that Dad had been really upset at the time.

The mist gave way to a downpour and we had to run back to the cars. I wasn't sorry. I didn't want to talk any more.

I drove home, parked the car and noticed that Dad was still in his office. He raised his head as I opened his door. 'Give me a couple of minutes,' he said.

I plonked myself down in his uncomfortable leather chair, wondering if this was the one for clients who defaulted on their bills. Otherwise his office was warm and pleasant, but I sensed something different. I glanced around. It was just too formal. There was no sign of his golf putter and balls which he used for relaxation at odd moments during the day. Maybe that was why I thought he looked tired and tense.

'How did the meeting go?' I could contain my curiosity no longer.

'Peter read a statement, signed by Jeffrey, stating that Alexander James Falkin was his son. Attached to it was a copy of a birth certificate. Plus there was a Trust document in his name and Alex Falkin produced his passport,' His tone was crisp.

'Was the name of his mother on the certificate?' I asked.

'The name Jane Oldman is on the certificate. According to Alexander Falkin it is false.'

'False?' I sat up.

'Once he knew he'd been adopted, he tried to trace her, unknown to Jeffrey, it seems. No record of her at all, either in Arizona or any other state,' his voice was still cold precision.

'That doesn't look good for him,' I said.

'No — and he refuses to give a DNA sample.'

I told Dad about meeting Alex on Ben Broar. 'He told me he wasn't prepared to go through with the test.'

'Evelyn and Steven aren't prepared to

accept his claim,' Dad said. 'They claim that passports can be forged, etc.'

'Alex says all he wants is to be acknowledged as Jeffrey's son. He's not interested in any inheritance,' I told him.

'Then why is he hanging around?' Dad almost barked.

That was so out of character, I almost forgot Alex's reason.

'Well, the funeral,' I said after a moment.

'Humph.' Was his reply.

I remembered Sarah's call. 'Jeffrey's sister might know something about him,' I said.

Suddenly Dad got up. 'This is Falkin business, Lizanne. What else is to come out if Jeffrey could keep a son hidden for thirty years? I'm weary of the whole thing. I'll be at the golf club for the rest of the evening,' he nodded at me, collected his jacket and left the office.

I sat in the chair, completely stunned. Whatever had got into Dad? Usually he enjoyed discussing a subject, sometimes even relishing a bit of gossip. I didn't understand Dad's reaction at all.

Rather wearily I went up to my flat, stripped off my damp clothes and cobbled together a light meal. I wouldn't see Steven tonight, much as I might want to. He would stay and keep Evelyn company and that was the right thing to do.

I rang him to pass on Sarah's reminder. 'No, I haven't forgotten, love,' he said. 'I'll pick you up about nine in the morning.'

The 'love' told me he'd got over his anger at my taking Alex to the hotel. I was relieved. Steven came first with me and I didn't want that to be threatened.

'Dad tells me it was a fraught meeting this morning,' I said. No way would I tell him that I'd heard most of it from Alex. It had been an unplanned meeting with him, but I sensed Steven might put a wrong interpretation on it.

'Nothing was resolved,' he said tersely.

I didn't ask any more. I suspected

that Evelyn was sitting in the solar close by and he wouldn't voice his true feelings.

It was only the following morning that I remembered Alex mentioning Jeffrey had told him about the business meeting in Aberdeen and that I'd meant to pass that on to Steven. He had a right to know. After all, he was surely in charge of Falkin Freight now.

'Something Alex Falkin said the other day,' I began vaguely as the car approached the Erskine Bridge on the way to Glasgow Airport. 'Your father told him he was fitting in a business meeting before picking him up at the airport in Aberdeen.'

'A meeting with whom?' Steven asked.

'I don't think he said and, anyway, it probably wouldn't mean anything to Alex.'

'Maybe not, Lizanne,' Steven said after a moment. 'On the other hand, if he is an impostor and after an inheritance, I would have thought he'd take care to research everything he could about the family and the business. I can't think of any business associate in Aberdeen, but I'll check that out with the office. It's time I took charge there anyway.'

'Your Aunt Sarah said something odd,' I went on, determined to give him all the information I had. 'Peter Clark doesn't hold your father's will.'

'So I discovered yesterday,' Steven's voice was grim. 'He would say nothing more on the subject when I challenged him, only that he'd have it in his hands soon.'

At that point we were approaching the entrance to the airport so I didn't bother to mention that Aunt Sarah had been surprised that the funeral was so soon. Anyway, that was something she could discuss with Evelyn and Steven.

Once the announcement went up that the plane had landed we went over to the arrivals hall.

I wondered if she had Jeffrey's will. But if so, why? I didn't think she'd be a legatee, although she might own some shares in the company. I remembered Steven telling me about a holiday he'd spent with her some years ago and describing the lavish set up — a ranch house, with a string of horses, the ubiquitous swimming pool, etc.

Then a sneaky thought crept into my mind. Maybe Jeffrey had left her some money — a reward for loyal silence about his real reason for visiting Arizona? Of course, all this mean speculation rested on Alex Falkin being exactly who he said he was.

'Here she is,' Steven said and walked forward to meet his aunt.

She was vaguely familiar to me — a smallish woman, trim figure, neat hair discreetly coloured, wearing pastels and grey cleverly blended in a two-piece light-weight outfit. She saw Steven and waved, a small smile lighting an otherwise controlled face. That was the only resemblance to Jeffrey.

I held back as they exchanged private words and then they began to walk towards me. Sarah would have walked right past me had Steven not caught her arm.

'Aunt Sarah, Lizanne came to meet you too, here she is,' he said, halting her walk.

Sarah had not noticed me, probably still lost in her thoughts of Jeffrey, I surmised. But when she turned to face me a range of expressions chased across the small face and it struggled to regain its composure.

Surprise I expected, but consternation and evasion too? I was at a complete loss as to how to interpret her reaction.

4

I kept quiet on the return journey to Gilliestoun as Sarah didn't even try to engage me in conversation. I wondered if her feelings about me were similar to Jeffrey's — polite courtesy at arms' length. Another puzzle as she scarcely knew me.

There was a soft murmur of words between her and Steven, but I switched off. I had something else to think about, anyway. On the earliest part of our journey to the airport, Steven told me about his visit to the Broq company in Rotterdam.

'It was humiliating,' he began. 'They had been expecting Dad, of course. I explained that Mr Falkin had gone to the States. Then they welcomed me.'

'How was that humiliating?' I asked.

'They addressed me as Mr Wallace,' Steven said grimly.

'You mean as in Evan Wallace?'

Wallace was Jeffrey's manager at the Falkin Freight depot and technically third in command.

'Exactly. And they were unaware that I was in fact a Falkin. They didn't know Dad had a son in the company,' he gave a harsh laugh. 'I wonder what they'd say if they knew he had another one!'

I ignored that. 'Anyway, once you'd told them who you were — ' I began.

'They asked a few tentative questions and when it became clear I didn't know what they were talking about, they clammed up.'

'What d'you mean?' I was confused.

'Something's going on between Broq and our company,' he said. 'They sussed pretty quickly that I was in the dark and promptly said they'd postpone the discussion until Dad was able to visit them.'

'You mean only your Dad and Evan Wallace know what the business is,' I deduced.

'Exactly. Can you imagine how

stupid I felt? On paper I'm Dad's second in command. In reality, I've just been the tea boy.' There was real bitterness in his tone.

It was an over-exaggeration, but I knew Steven had always resented the fact that Jeffrey had insisted he joined the business straight after college. Jeffrey had paid him a good salary, with perks, but never given him any responsibility.

'Well, you have to remind everyone that you are in charge of Falkin Freight now and it's up to Wallace to come clean with you,' I pointed out.

'How do you know that I'm in charge of Falkin Freight? Given what we've learned in the last few days, Dad could have willed the business away from me completely.'

'No, he wouldn't do that to you,' I tried comforting him, although not entirely sure that my words had any certainty. Last week there would have been no question. There was definitely another son, proof lay in Peter Clark's files, but whether it was this Alex who'd turned up or not, the reality was another possible heir.

When we arrived at Gilliestoun I said polite goodbyes to Steven and Sarah and went into my museum. It was an oasis of calm which I needed just at that moment, although I knew it was going to be some time before I could put all my thoughts in any sort of order. I didn't even get a minute.

Christina Dunure breezed in and threw herself down on the chair. 'I came by to give my condolences to Jeffrey's sister. Do you know if she has arrived by now?' she asked.

'Yes, Steven and I met her at the airport. They've just gone into the Tower.'

'Right, I'd better go and see her,' she heaved herself out of the chair then turned to me. 'Something else I meant to say to you, seems to have slipped my mind,' Christina pulled at the embroidery on her sweat shirt. 'So many worries at the moment, Lizzie, the farm and everything,' her voice trailed off.

I felt concern for her. She had handed over the running of the farm to Todd when her husband had died, only keeping her piggery. Despite Todd's professed love of the land I'd never pegged him as being a good farmer. It would break Christina's heart if he'd let things slide out of control.

'Oh, it's come back to me,' she said as she reached the door. 'I was here earlier to see Sarah and ran into that new chap. Alex Falkin he calls himself. He was looking for you. Asked me to tell you to phone him,' and with that she strode out of the barn.

Why me, I wondered? What could Alex Falkin want with me?

I presumed he was at the hotel, so I rang there and was put through to his room.

'Something I'd like to show you,' he said tersely after the barest of greetings. 'Can we meet at yesterday's place?'

'I haven't any transport,' I said. 'Don't come to the museum. I'll start walking and you can pick me up on the road. Fifteen minutes.'

He agreed and rang off. It seemed pathetically cloak and dagger, but I really did not want to be seen with Alex. News would soon get back to Steven and I didn't want that. I was also a little wary that Alex was attempting to recruit me as a foot soldier in support of his campaign to be recognised as Jeffrey's son. I had been hospitable and friendly towards him, mainly in the absence of such overtures from the Falkins, but I definitely wasn't taking sides.

Fortunately no-one was around when he stopped the car on the hilly road leading to Ben Broar and I jumped in at once.

He said nothing until he'd parked where I'd found him the day before. Then he reached into his pocket and took out an envelope.

'This was left at reception for me just after breakfast,' he said.

It was a plain white A4 envelope,

typical office stationary with ALEX FALKIN written in biro on the front. I opened it and took out a sheet of paper, same quality as the envelope. The message was brief.

Leave Scotland now or take the consequences.

There was no address, date or signature. 'For heaven's sake,' I cried. 'Who sent you this rubbish?'

'On the face of it,' Alex said coldly, 'it looks like a schoolboy joke, but then what schoolboys know about me?'

'This is the work of a mischief maker and can't be taken seriously,' I was furious that someone in Drumbroar had acted like this.

'But why send it now?' He made a grimace. 'It isn't as if anyone here actually believes I am Jeffrey's son. I'm hardly a threat to anyone.'

'A threat?' I asked.

'Well, that's what I think this note suggests. 'Take the consequences' surely means I could find myself up against trouble of some kind,' he said.

'For what reason?' I was truly puzzled.

'Only thing I can think of is the matter of inheritance,' he replied.

'That supposes the contents of Jeffrey's will are known.'

'Which seems to be impossible as Peter Clark says he doesn't have it,' he pointed out.

'Unless someone in the family knows what Jeffrey intended,' I said.

'Definitely not. Evelyn, Steven and Julia made that quite clear by their behaviour. If it contains anything to benefit me they are going to fight it,' he said grimly.

'That's only because they're not sure you are Jeffrey's son,' I reminded him. 'By the way his sister, Sarah, has arrived.'

'Does that have any significance?'

I shrugged. 'When I spoke to her on the phone the other day, she knew that Peter Clark didn't have the will, so I assume she knows where it is.'

'Like she has been holding it?' he

73

asked, quick as a flash.

I shrugged, but I'd been playing with that thought since her phone call.

'So if no-one actually knows yet what's in it, who has a motive to get rid of me?' he said it lightly, but his eyes were questioning.

'Well, it seems to be stretching the imagination that the family would threaten you with 'consequences'. Maybe the note was just to scare you off in case there is a legal battle,' I suggested.

'So the family might have a motive?' he asked.

'And then there's me,' I said.

He looked startled. 'You?'

'Mmm, more than anything I'd like to get my hands on Gilliestoun again,' I confessed.

He stared at me. 'But one thing is certain, Jeffrey won't have left it to me. And, more to the point, you wouldn't catch me using cheap notepaper like that.' I smiled at him.

He laughed then. I made to hand over the note.

'No, you told me that you're the investigator in this neck of the woods. I hereby hire you to find out who wrote that note,' he said. 'Without telling anyone else about it, of course.' He started the car and we drove back to Drumbroar.

★ ★ ★

I shopped for food in town then went home, all the time my mind concentrating on that note. The one person I wanted to confide in was Dad, but I had to respect Alex's wish to keep the note's existence secret. I decided my main line of enquiry had to be centred on whatever person expected to gain most from Jeffrey's will.

I knew Steven would not have stooped to anonymous threatening notes, but a little alarm bell had gone off in my head earlier at Christina's comment that she had so many worries, including the farm. Maybe Todd was in serious financial difficulties and was depending on Julia's inheritance from Jeffrey.

Instead of money going two ways between Steven and Julia, there could be a three-way split if Alex was included in the will, meaning less for all concerned. An anonymous note would be Todd's style.

I was trying to dismiss this as a vile and uncharitable thought when my phone rang. It was Dad, asking to come in for a cup of tea. I agreed at once, having been concerned at his obvious need to escape from me the day before.

'Sarah arrive OK?' he asked, standing beside me as I filled the kettle.

'Yes, fine.'

'What did she have to say?' he was watching me intently.

'Nothing to me, actually,' I said, switching on the gas. 'She seemed a little withdrawn, maybe the loss of Jeffrey is hitting her now that she's here.'

Dad moved to sit at the kitchen table. 'Did she mention Jeffrey's newfound son?' he asked sharply.

'Not when I was present,' I said, putting a couple of mugs on the table. 'But I should imagine she knows about him.'

'What makes you say that?' again his tone was sharp.

I shrugged. 'Remember that Jeffrey went to visit her in Arizona every six months or so. According to Alex, Jeffrey met him in Tucson as regular as that. So, if any of the family here had phoned Sarah in Phoenix to speak to Jeffrey, she must have had a cover story ready.'

'Mmm, that's a good point,' Dad conceded.

We sat quietly for a while, drinking the tea. 'I've been wondering if Sarah has had Jeffrey's will all along,' I said.

'It seems the only answer since Peter Clark doesn't have it,' he replied.

'I don't suppose you've any guesses as to how Jeffrey might have disposed of his worldly goods?' I asked.

'You know Jeffrey never confided in me, Lizanne. But this cuckoo in the nest could upset the apple-cart for Julia and Todd,' he said.

I stared at him. 'Did you know that Christina is worried about the farm?'

'With due cause,' Dad said. 'The whisper in town is that Todd is badly in debt. He's desperate to lay his hands on cash. Knowing him, I expect he's tried all the over and under-hand avenues already.'

★ ★ ★

Calm, sunny weather, heralded the morning of Jeffrey's funeral.

Dad and I arrived at the church early, but I noticed that Alex was already seated mid-way down the nave. From the hunch of his shoulders and the rigidity of his neck muscles, I sensed he wanted to sit alone.

We took a pew not far behind the one reserved for the family. Evelyn and Julia were elegant and dignified in black, but I could tell from his body language that Steven was tense.

Dad, beside me, was buttoned up. While he'd liked Jeffrey, they had never been close, so I rather thought he was living again the ordeal of Mother's funeral. He had never got over the loss.

At the graveside, Alex stood across from the family. His face was closed and unreadable as the last blessing was spoken and the coffin was lowered to rest.

Steven still looked bereft and I longed to comfort him, but his place was with Evelyn, his aunt and his sister. Just before they left, he turned and gave Alex a small nod.

'Did you see that?' I murmured to Dad, striving to keep the surprise from my voice.

'What?' was his terse response.

'Steven acknowledged Alex. They must now believe he is really Jeffrey's son.'

'I'm going home. I can't face the wake. Make my apologies.' Dad left my side before I could answer.

For a few moments I couldn't move,

so sudden and surprising was Dad's departure. I had thought we would visit my mother's grave.

As the funeral cars made their way from the cemetery I walked along the path and stood looking at mother's headstone for a moment. Then I heard a movement behind me.

'I thought your father was with you,' Alex said.

I shook my head. 'Funerals upset him and I think he wants to be alone with his memories of my mother.' I gestured to the headstone. 'He couldn't even bear to come here today.'

Alex read the inscription. 'Ten years ago. You must have been quite young.'

'Fifteen.'

He said nothing and I thought how selfish I was. He'd scarcely known his father for the first fifteen years.

'I'm so sorry, you have your own grief today,' I apologised.

'Yeah, the father who almost never was. There are so many thing that I'll never know now,' then his tone changed. 'Can we walk to Gilliestoun from here?'

'There's a path behind the church.' I gave a farewell bow to Mother's headstone and then left the churchyard with Alex.

When we arrived at the Tower, Bess was by the oak door, directing guests up to the solar. Dressed in black, she was a more sombre version of the Bess I knew. Her face showed genuine compassion when she saw Alex.

'He was a grand man,' she murmured to him and he stopped to shake her hand, clearly moved by her words.

My thoughts flew back to the moment at the graveside when Steven had nodded at Alex. Now Bess was apparently accepting Alex as Jeffrey's son. There could only be one explanation. Sarah must have confirmed it.

Any doubts I might have had were banished when Evelyn indicated that Alex should stand in line with her, Steven and Julia, to receive the condolences. They were ranged just below my grandmother's portrait, facing the guests.

Evelyn actually introduced Alex to everyone. 'This is Alex, Jeffrey's son, who lives in America,' she said.

It must have cost her dear, but she sounded gracious and dignified and I admired her.

My eyes raked over the guests wondering who had sent that threatening note to Alex. The writer clearly believed Alex was genuine, but how could he have known? Sarah hadn't arrived until after the note had been delivered.

I helped Bess with serving the food and drinks. I knew Evelyn would expect me to, but I didn't mind in the least. I eavesdropped on as many conversations as possible as I circulated, but while the gossip about Alex was all speculation, no-one was giving anything away.

Eventually people began to form into groups and I found Alex by my side. 'I need some fresh air,' he murmured.

'Would you like to go on to the roof?' I asked.

He didn't respond. There were far fewer people in the solar now and he was able to take in all the glory of the room. His head was held high, fixed rather, and I realised he was looking at the portrait of my grandmother, which he obviously hadn't noticed before. He looked quite stunned and I wasn't surprised. It was a magnificent piece of art, life size and executed by a renowned Scottish painter.

'My grandmother, Elizabeth Anne,' I said with pride.

He continued to stare without comment.

'I don't know what happened to the best genes when they reached my generation,' I said lightly. 'I turned out to be rather a raw-boned galumph.'

I expected him to question my 'galumph' but there was no humour in his eyes.

'What about your mother? Did she

inherit your grandmother's looks?' he asked.

I laughed. 'Oh yes, all the beauty and the grace. She was the image of her mother, Elizabeth Anne, and a warm person as well. I wish you had met her, you'd have liked her.'

I now had all his attention and there was sympathy in his eyes, together with another expression which I couldn't read. 'You miss her, just as much as Hamish does,' he said quietly.

I couldn't hold his gaze as my throat was threatening to close with emotion. I too had never got over losing her.

He looked at the portrait again. 'Why don't you and Hamish have the portrait?' he asked.

'This is its rightful place,' I said simply, my voice steady again.

'Did my father ask for it to remain in the solar?'

'He suggested it, more I think to soften the blow of our losing Gilliestoun, as if a little bit of my history still lived here,' I said.

'Right, let's explore,' Alex said briskly as if he'd had enough of the subject.

We climbed the spiral staircase and emerged on to the roof. Alex walked around clearly impressed by the extensive views over Loch Broar, the town and the mountains in the distance.

I was dying to ask him if indeed Sarah had confirmed his true identity, but it seemed crude and invasive at the moment. So I did a little sneaky thing.

'Quite an inheritance, isn't it?' I said, not stipulating whether I meant his or mine.

'Not any use to me,' he said harshly. 'Bricks and mortar take too long to convert to cash. And that's what I need.'

I stared at him.

'I wasn't lying when I said I wanted to come here to meet the family,' he continued. 'But more than anything, I wanted Dad to help me sort myself out. I wanted to discuss what to do with the rest of my life, with his support if necessary. I spent my last cent coming here, Lizanne. I am completely broke.'

5

My first thought was to wonder if all Jeffrey's plans were turning to ashes. No doubt he had intended well by his sons, so were they incapable of emulating his success or had he failed to see that they definitely weren't chips off the old block? Had he been blind to the fact that they needed to establish their own paths through life? Had he denied Alex any opportunity hoping that in the end he would become part of Falkin Freight just as Steven had been forced to be? In the short time I'd known Alex, I suspected he would never settle to work for a freight company.

'I meant to ask before,' I said casually. 'When did you change your name to Falkin?'

'When I was twenty-one — an attempt to get Dad to really acknowledge me,' he replied. 'My adoptive parents didn't seem to mind or perhaps I was just too insensitive to see it,' he sounded genuinely regretful.

'When did you become interested in photography?'

'Travelling around the States.' He didn't seem to resent my questions. 'There are so many places where you are silenced by the grandeur or quirkiness or sheer scale of nature's achievements. Somehow I wanted to record them — just for myself, not for personal gain,' he replied.

'Maybe you can make a fresh start here with photographs of Scotland?' I said lightly.

'More than just a little hobby for a bum?' he retorted.

'Sorry, that sounded patronising,' I apologised. Alex had gone through quite enough today without my thoughtlessness.

He laughed. 'Forget it, Lizanne, you speak as you think and I'm getting used to it.'

We were suddenly joined on the roof

by Steven and Todd. They both looked startled when they saw us and stopped their conversation at once. Steven sent me a cool look. In return I gave him one of my special smiles but it spectacularly failed to register. Surely he wasn't jealous of Alex? He was completely natural with him, however.

'Hi,' he said to his brother. 'Getting a breath of fresh air?'

'Yeah and one spectacular view,' Alex replied.

'Of course, this landscape will be completely foreign to you,' Todd drawled.

'Getting to know it,' Alex replied, refusing to rise to the bait.

'I'm glad about that,' Steven said. 'After all, you're half a Scot.'

There was just the tiniest hesitation then Alex nodded. 'So it seems,' his light tone sounded a trifle strained.

'Actually, Peter Clark wants us all down in the solar for the reading of the will now that everyone but family has left,' Steven said. Again he glanced at me.

'OK, I'll leave you to it,' I picked up the message.

'Can you switch our phones through to the barn, we don't want to be disturbed,' Steven said.

'Sure,' I slipped behind the three men and made my way downstairs, my mind buzzing. How I wished I could be a fly on the wall in the solar. But I knew I had to distance myself from the Falkins over this. What Jeffrey had done with his money was their business, not mine. I had a 5% holding of Falkin shares which was inviolable.

When I reached the kitchen, Bess was busy tidying up with the help of three local girls so I wasn't needed.

Back in the museum I naturally couldn't sit still. I paced up and down occasionally glancing out of the window at Gilliestoun. If Steven was successful in gaining control of the company what would he do?

On the other hand what if Steven wanted to sell the company? Would he leave Gilliestoun? And if the company was sold would Evelyn be able to afford to live there without the company income? Would Gilliestoun have to be sold?

I felt a shiver of premonition about the future. It had been bad enough giving up the Tower to Jeffrey and family, but I didn't think I could bear to see it in the hands of complete strangers.

I almost jumped out of my skin when the telephone rang. The museum was officially closed so it couldn't be a client. Then I remembered switching the Tower phone through to mine as Steven had asked.

'Gilliestoun Tower,' I said, thinking the phone call had to be for someone there. I was right.

'I'd like to speak to a Mr Falkin,' the voice was male, cultured, but certainly not on the young side.

'I'm afraid he's engaged on business at the moment, can I take a message?' I said in my best secretary manner.

'Well, it is rather difficult. First of all

90

I wanted to pass on my condolences on the loss of his father, Jeffrey. I read of his death in my local paper only today. The accident must have happened just after he left my home,' he said.

My investigative antenna sparked up immediately.

'Do I understand you live near Aberdeen?' I asked.

'Yes, near Banchory in the county of Aberdeenshire. I'm Fergus McLachlan of Skirl House.' This time the tone was slightly puzzled.

'Oh, yes, of course,' I bluffed a little. 'The family didn't know Jeffrey had gone to Aberdeenshire,' I explained a trifle lamely. 'His original intention had been to travel to the United States.'

'Yes. I know that,' the reply was a touch testy. 'Of course when his son decided to come to Scotland instead, that all changed.'

I was too shocked to respond. Here was someone outside the family who had been told about Alex.

'Perhaps you'd ask one of Jeffrey's

sons to contact me with regard to the business dealings I was discussing with Jeffrey? I think it is rather more urgent now, don't you agree?' Mr McLachlan said.

I hadn't the faintest clue what he was talking about, but I wasn't going to let on, especially as I didn't think Steven knew of this. But perhaps Alex did?

'If I could explain, Mr McLachlan,' I said. 'Mr Falkin's funeral has just taken place today and the family is at this moment at a business meeting. I'll speak to both men as soon as possible.'

'Of course. My apologies for intruding at this time. Had I known of Jeffrey's death I would, of course, have attended the funeral,' the reprimand was there in his voice.

Hurriedly I said, 'If I may just take your telephone number? Matters are a little confused at the moment.'

If he was surprised he didn't show it, just gave a note of his phone number and then rang off.

I was glad I'd had the wit to ask for

it, although I would have remembered *Skirl House.* It had the ring of somewhere important. Somehow I didn't think Steven knew of this man or for that matter did anyone else in the family, otherwise I would have been asked to notify Mr McLachlan of Jeffrey's accident. Also, had the family known of him, it wouldn't have come as such a surprise that Jeffrey had gone to Aberdeenshire.

As I replaced the phone I looked out of the window again just in time to see the Tower's heavy oak door flung open and Steven hurtle out. He took the path that led behind the Tower and down to Loch Broar.

I caught up with him as fast as I could. He turned when he heard my running steps. His colour was high, his jaw set and his eyes dark with fury.

'He can't do it! He can't control me from the grave,' his voice was raw with bitterness. 'I won't have it. He can't do this to me!'

I'd never seen Steven like this before.

I said nothing, sick with anticipation at the same time. Just what had Jeffrey's will contained?

He attacked a tree next then whirled to face me again. 'Oh, a fair division — I'll give him that — to include my new brother, which we had to expect,' he suddenly pointed the stick at me and his words were icy with precise enunciation. 'No inheritance, nothing from the company if we sell it. The money will go to the workers to set up a public company for them.'

I was horrified! Jeffrey could not have done this! By denying him money from any sale, he had tied Steven to the company forever, denied him the chance of following his own course in life, as he could do nothing without capital.

'And, he's made me managing director — a toy title — a sop for the yes-man. Did he despise me that much?' Steven flung himself along the path again. I didn't follow him. There was absolutely nothing I could say to make it better. I'd have to leave it until later to tell him about Mr McLachlan.

I trudged back to the museum, collected my belongings and left.

Back home, I went straight to Dad's door and knocked loudly. He opened it after a minute or so and I noticed at once that he looked drawn. He invited me in, offered me a drink and sat down. He didn't ask about the wake. I didn't say anything. I thought my earlier guess had been correct. Memories of Mother's funeral were still strong and I doubted if he'd entered Gilliestoun in years. Even a glimpse of Grandmother's portrait would have been painful to him. It was strange how it had impressed Alex. Probably his first encounter with a visual tradition. I had never known my grandmother, and so for Dad and me the portrait was just like looking at a picture of mother.

I decided to concentrate on the will. And, if possible, find out more. 'Steven is in a fine state,' I said.

Dad frowned. 'What about? If you

mean his inheritance, it seemed to me a fair distribution of Jeffrey's assets.'

'You do know all the details then?'

He gave me an old-fashioned look. 'Yes, Peter Clark went over them with me this morning. He wanted me there at Gilliestoun, but I declined.'

'When did Jeffrey write this will?' was my next question.

'It was dated five years ago,' Dad said.

Just about the time Steven had started work with the company. 'And I take it that Alex's legality was confirmed?'

Dad gave me an irritated look which I felt was unjustified.

'Yes, Sarah confirmed it. She had brought a sheaf of photographs, plus the will from Arizona. The photographs showed Jeffrey and Alex together over the years. There is no doubt as to Alex's claim to be his son.'

'Why did she have the will?' I asked.

'Sarah said it was a form of insurance, so that if anything should happen to Jeffrey, it would act as proof to substantiate Alex's claim. In other words, the will's terms would only be valid if Alex was acknowledged.'

It made sense. 'Why did she want to delay the funeral?'

'She was unaware that Alex was already in Scotland and was trying to contact him in Tucson. His adoptive parents told her where he was.'

That sorted out that little mystery for me, but I still wanted more discussion on the will. 'Do you really think that Jeffrey should have restricted Steven — and Alex — from selling Falkin Freight?'

Dad shrugged. 'Maybe he was thinking of all the people here in Drumbroar who would be out of work if the company was to move away.'

'Steven would not have dealt with it that way,' I said. 'He would have made sure that no-one was made redundant.'

Dad didn't look in the least interested. And then I got to the question that had been burning inside me.

'Who inherits Gilliestoun?'

He looked away from me. 'Steven and Alex have joint ownership.'

I was absolutely astounded. 'Alex! He's joint owner? But he's never had anything to do with Gilliestoun. Had no real idea of what it was like until he got here!'

Dad got up from his chair, moved to the window and stared out, his back to me. He clearly didn't want to discuss that aspect, perhaps for my sake.

'What about Julia?' I asked.

'She's inherited a small legacy and some shares in the company. Presumably Jeffrey thought that having a husband and a home was security enough for her.'

'Isn't that going to be a blow for her and Todd?' I asked.

'I should imagine so,' Dad sounded completely weary.

It was so unlike him. Normally he was interested in all the fine details of inheritances and had often helped me on occasion when I'd been hired to investigate dodgy wills.

'Any other legacies?' I asked casually.

He detailed them in a monotone voice, some to cousins whom I took to be Alex's adoptive parents, plus shares for Sarah. I wondered if she was being rewarded for her silence over Alex.

'You'll have to excuse me, Lizanne. I'm going out now,' Dad said.

'Sure.' I smiled, but inwardly I was distressed. Whatever was the matter with him? He never behaved like this.

Since we'd always been so close, I knew better than to fuss. He would tell me whatever was bugging him when he was ready. I went next door to my own flat.

I'd barely finished a meal when my telephone rang. 'Lizanne, I need some help.' It was Alex.

'With what?' I said, thinking of the threatening note he'd received. I'd been unable to discover anything about the sender.

'A place of my own.'

'Here in Drumbroar?'

'Got it in one.'

'What are you going to do for money?' I blurted out the question without thinking.

'You do go for the jugular, don't you?' Alex laughed loudly. 'Haven't you heard? I'm now joint owner of Falkin Freight, position not yet decided, but there should be a salary in there somewhere.'

'So . . . you mean . . . you're staying on in Scotland?'

'The perceptive detective at work again,' he teased. 'Now, I fancy a cottage, somewhere with a good roof, loads of character and easy to run. Any ideas?'

I was about to answer when the intercom rang. At this hour? 'Hang on,' I said to Alex and walked over to the window which looked over the street. Steven stood outside. I could tell immediately from his body language that he was tense and angry. I had a fair idea what was behind that.

'Got a visitor. I'll ring you back later,'

I said to Alex and disconnected.

A few minutes later I opened the door to Steven. 'Alone, are you?' were his words of greeting.

'Yes, Dad's gone out,' I replied smoothly, not rising to the bait.

'I didn't mean your father and you know that, Lizanne. I thought you might have had my brother here. You seem to be close.'

'Don't be tiresome, Steven,' I said, walking away and leaving him to close the door.

He followed me into my living-room. 'He can't keep away from you and it's obvious you have a lot of time for him!' he accused me.

'Well, nobody else had until today,' I flashed back. 'Somebody had to talk to him.'

'Talk to him! Is that all it is? Are you going to ditch me for my older brother?' Steven's face was dull red.

I handed him a glass of malt whisky which he raised to his mouth immediately.

'You must think me very shallow if I could change allegiance within a couple of days of meeting the man,' I was determined to play this as cool as possible.

'But you fancy him, don't you?'

I strove to keep hold of my temper. Steven would not normally have used cheap language like that. I had to remember just what he'd gone through in the last few days.

'No, Steven. I don't fancy Alex. He appears to be an ordinary guy who has had a rough ride recently, maybe even all his life. He needed someone to talk to these last few days, that's all it was.'

'Well, it doesn't look that way to everyone else,' Steven's voice still had a rough edge. 'And you were showing him all over Gilliestoun. Did you expect him to inherit it, being the eldest son?'

'That's not worthy of you, Steven. I've never concealed the fact that I like to think I still belong in Gilliestoun, but I won't use anyone to get there. Not even you!'

'That's not what everyone thinks,' he retorted, helping himself to more whisky.

Now I did get angry. 'Everyone? And who might they be? And when did you begin listening to them instead of me!'

'Gossip about you and him is rife in Drumbroar,' he mumbled.

'I expect gossip is rife about Alex in Drumbroar and, sadly, your father too, Steven, and whoever might have been Alex's mother. That will take up far more attention than any part I might have.' I drew a deep breath. 'I suggest you sort that out before coming here and accusing me of nothing more than being a civil person.'

'I don't want you seeing Alex again,' he shouted at me.

I reckoned it was more bluster than anything else, but my temper was running out of control now.

'Just go, Steven. This conversation is at an end.' I took the glass from his hand and went pointedly to the door.

'I knew it! There's something going

on between you. You'd better sort yourself out, Lizanne. I won't stand for this!' He flung himself out of the door.

I followed him down the stairs, planning to say a few calming words when we reached the front door, but we both froze on the doorstep.

Alex's car was parked outside and he was emerging from it. Without a word Steven made off down the street. Alex just caught a glimpse of his retreating back then turned a questioning eye on me.

'Let's just say bad timing,' I sighed. 'Come up.'

Inside the flat, I held up my hands. 'I haven't had time to think about a place for you to rent,' I said, rather weary of the Falkin family.

Immediately I took in his grim expression.

'Does the name Margaret Drummond mean anything to you?' he asked.

It was such an unexpected question that my mind momentarily went blank.

'Margaret Drummond? No, I don't

know of anyone by that name.'

'Think hard, Lizanne. I reckon she must be a woman in her mid-fifties.'

'I can't say I know everyone in this town, but Drummond isn't a common name here,' I told him.

'It could possibly be a maiden name,' he said.

'It would take some digging to check all the maiden names in this town. Who is she anyway?' I asked.

'Claims she's my mother.'

'What?' I almost shrieked. That was the last thing I'd expected. Now I could see why he was so wrought up. 'But she can't be. I thought your mother was dead!'

He flung himself down on my sofa. 'Exactly.'

I noticed then that he held an envelope in his hand. 'Another letter?' I felt uneasy.

He passed it over to me. I saw at once that this one was unlike the threatening note. The paper and envelope were of much better quality and the writing, in a bold hand, was entirely different, quite distinctive in fact.

It was simply headed: *Drumbroar* and the day's date.

I read: *I am writing to advise you that you are my son, Alexander James Falkin. I should like us to meet*

Yours sincerely, Margaret Drummond.

6

I sat for a long time after Alex left. I needed some quiet reflective moments to examine all that had happened since the day we heard Jeffrey had died. Life had hurtled on at such a pace that so much had become muddled and confused. It left me feeling out of synch. I'd always wanted my life to be ordered, but it was a faint hope at the best of times.

Most of all I needed time to sort out my feelings, in particular towards Steven and Alex. Steven was naturally uppermost in my mind. We'd always known each other, being brought up in the same town and with the Gilliestoun connection. He is two years older than me, but our friendship really began when I left school.

I accepted Steven's anger at my friendship with Alex. It probably looked in the beginning like something of a betrayal in the particular circumstances. But a curl of uncertainty lurked inside me now. The part of our row that referred to Gilliestoun seemed to expose an underlying suspicion of Steven's — that gaining possession of the Tower was my priority in life — and that I'd use anyone to achieve it.

Basically, I had befriended Alex for the simple reason that no-one else had. I had recognised the bewilderment of bereavement he was experiencing when we first met. I had been there with the loss of my mother and it had been second nature to take him under my wing — if that is what I did.

Now there was the appearance of this letter. Alex had flung it down on my table before he left with the words: 'You have records of everyone in this town, find out who she is.'

I studied the letter analytically. The style was formal with no grammatical or spelling errors, but it was hardly the letter of a mother to a long-lost son. The writing itself was interesting

— bold diagonal lettering, but with jagged breaks in each word. Its appearance seemed familiar to me, yet out of place in the circumstances. Maybe I'd come across it in the course of my work, but it must have been a long time ago.

It was certainly completely different from the earlier, threatening note Alex had been sent. It didn't seem possible that the two could be linked.

'She knows your full name,' I commented.

He shrugged. 'It's on my papers, anyone could find that out. But that's not important. Her claim is false. She is not my mother,' he stated.

'How can you be so certain? I admit the tone is rather distant, but she must have found it difficult to write.'

'I'm certain. I may not have a drop of American blood in my veins, but she is not my mother,' his tone bristled with finality.

'Then forget it. Some crank,' I said.

'Not altogether,' he passed me the

envelope, turning it over to display the back with the message in the same handwriting'

I have also written to Peter Clark.

This put a completely different complexion on it. This woman was prepared to go public.

'I reckon she's after money. After all, I've been here for several days and she hadn't bothered to contact me until now,' Alex said.

'She's assuming Jeffrey left you some.'

Alex almost smiled. 'She's in for a shock, isn't she? Not a cent, just a voice in the business.'

I ventured the next suggestion cautiously. 'Perhaps she thinks you will sell your share of Gilliestoun.'

'How do you know I inherited half of that?' His voice was smoothly questioning.

'I asked my father in a roundabout way,' I confessed. 'To be fair, he thought Steven had told me, so he didn't think he was breaking any confidentiality rule.'

He returned to the subject of the letter. 'Has your dad ever mentioned Jeffrey being friendly with any woman round here?'

'He can think of no-one,' I assured him, without thinking.

'So you have discussed the matter,' he said. 'I suppose that's only natural.'

'Yes, we did,' I told him frankly. 'But that was when you first arrived. Not since the reading of the will.'

'Has your father always lived in Drumbroar?' he asked then.

'He moved here from Stirling to take up his apprenticeship and met my mother and that was it. He never moved on.'

'I take it that their marriage was happy,' Alex said casually.

'Yes, it was and I had a good childhood,' I said.

'How did your mother feel about losing Gilliestoun?' he asked.

'That was before I was born. My grandparents moved to a villa in

Drumbroar and then my grandmother fell ill. My mother nursed her until she died. About a year later she married Dad. She never really mentioned the loss of the Tower. I presumed she wasn't as obsessed as me,' I shrugged. 'I'm a throwback to an earlier generation, wedded to the tradition. You must think me very odd, clinging on to tattered history.'

He was quiet for a moment, then said, 'If you had asked me last week I'd have said it was crazy trying to keep a place like Gilliestoun going against all the modern trends. But now I think it has a kind of grim charisma,' he paused. 'Maybe it's in the blood.'

I went back to the reason for his visit. 'Look, I'll ask Dad about Margaret Drummond.'

'Oh no, Lizanne, please don't bother him. She is not my mother and Peter Clark can sort out any claims she makes.'

He left then, throwing the letter on my table.

The first thing I remembered on waking the next day was that I had forgotten to tell Steven about Fergus McLachlan's telephone call.

I rang him immediately at Gilliestoun and relayed the details of the call from Skirl House.

'Too busy entertaining my brother to remember a simple message?' was his taut reply to my information.

'Don't be wearisome, Steven. Alex came to see me about something that could be significant. Had you waited he would have told you too,' I said.

'And what is it?'

'That's for him to tell you, not me,' I snapped. 'Anyway the important thing is that this Mr McLachlan wants to see both you and Alex as soon as possible about something he discussed with your father.'

'I'm flying to Rotterdam today to see what business Broq had with my father,' he said. 'I'm in charge now and that comes first. Why don't you take my brother to Aberdeenshire. That should please you both,' and he slammed the phone down.

I went straight to Dad's flat. 'Would it be possible for me to borrow your car today?' I asked.

'Yes, no problem,' he replied. 'I'm in the office all day.'

I was surprised he didn't seem in the least curious as to what I needed it for. As he handed over the keys, I said: 'Do you know anyone in Drumbroar called Margaret Drummond?'

'Can't say I do,' he said, uninterested.

'She'd be about your age and lived here for say, thirty years,' I pursued the matter.

'Still no. What's this about anyway?' he asked, pottering about his hall.

'She's written to Alex claiming to be his mother.'

He stopped dead in his tracks and stared at me. 'What?' his voice sounded faint with shock.

'She left a letter at Alex's hotel and says she's also written to Peter Clark.'

Dad smiled and I noticed tension

draining from his face. He took a deep breath. 'Ah, the first of many.'

'Fortune hunters?' I guessed.

'They all crawl out of the woodwork when there's a good will and especially in this case with the unknown quantity factor. I'm surprised that more of Jeffrey's sons haven't turned up.'

'Dad! Alex is for real,' I said.

'Yes, I know. Silly joke. We'll just have to scare this Margaret Drummond a little with charges of false pretences and so on.'

He sounded very jovial and I was puzzled by his sudden change of mood.

'She wants to meet him,' I said. 'And I wonder how she knows that Alex never knew his mother.'

'Gossip, my dear.' He ushered me out of his flat.

I drove as fast as the legal limit permitted but still I was too late to catch Steven before he left for the airport.

'Went down the drive, not ten minutes ago like a bat escaping hell,'

Bess told me when she answered the door to the Tower.

'Thanks, Bess. He's in a strop with me, a lot of it my fault, and I'm in a dilemma now,' I told her. I hesitated for a moment thinking I really should go back to Drumbroar and tell Alex about Fergus McLachlan. Surely it would do no harm if I went to Aberdeenshire with him? I felt obliged to follow up McLachlan's telephone call and confess my forgetfulness.

Then, out of the corner of my eye, I saw Steven's aunt, Sarah, walking in the grounds. She had been brought up in Drumbroar, she might well know this Margaret Drummond.

'I'm going to have a word with Sarah,' I said to Bess.

I caught up with her, noticing she was pale and that her eyes seemed drawn down at the corners. The expression in her eyes changed from weary to wary when she saw me. Why that again?

'Hi, how are you?' I asked, genuinely

concerned at her appearance.

'I guess I'm feeling worse than I did yesterday,' she said.

'I expect the reality will hit everyone here when the company has to get back to normal,' I sympathised.

Sarah made no comment on that and we continued walking for a while then she said, 'He was a fun brother when we grew up together. I didn't see much of him after I went to the States.' She paused and continued in a drier tone. 'I expect everyone has gathered that by now.'

I decided to take advantage of the opening Sarah had handed me. 'There must be lots of things you remember from your life here — ' I began.

'Yes, and most of them are private,' she cut me off.

I almost gasped at the speed and tone of her reply. What made her think I was prying? It was as if she had something to hide.

'Are you pumping me on Alex's behalf?' she said, completely taking the wind out of my sails.

'Partly, but he doesn't know,' I said flatly.

'Then what's this about?'

'A woman called Margaret Drummond wrote to Alex claiming to be his mother,' I gave it to her straight, watching closely.

At once the taut lines of her face relaxed. So that wasn't what she'd been expecting! I carried on, making my tone conversational, not confrontational. 'She appears to be a local woman and I was only going to ask if you remember her.'

'Can't say I do,' Sarah said casually. 'Sounds like someone just trying to jump on the bandwagon.'

How strange! Both Alex and Dad had said more or less the same thing as if all three knew Margaret Drummond definitely wasn't Alex's mother. Perhaps Sarah knew the identity of the mysterious missing Jane Oldman. Had she told Alex, but if so, why hadn't he told me?

We walked back in silence to the oak

door of the tower. 'Poor Jeffrey, he never intended to leave this mess behind,' Sarah said.

I'd had the same thought, so what had gone wrong? 'This woman says she is contacting Peter Clark, so no doubt he will deal with her,' I explained.

'I certainly hope so,' Sara said wearily.

'I'm sorry if I upset you,' I said. 'Alex asked me to investigate this woman. It's the sort of thing I do.'

'I remember when you were a kid you were always poking your nose into things. It seems you've found the right career,' she said, but her tone was jokey rather than angry.

I left Sarah and went over to my museum, my mind in a whirl. I made myself some instant coffee and sat down to analyse, if I could, what information I'd gleaned and where I went from here.

I was sorry that I'd missed Steven, although since he was booked to go to Rotterdam he wouldn't have been able to visit Fergus McLachlan.

Steven had suggested, albeit in a fit of pique, that I take Alex to Skirl House, but again I was uneasy about Alex. As far as I could see there was still an element of mystery about him. After my talk with Sarah, I was more than ever convinced that he wasn't telling me something.

Both Dad and Sarah had dismissed this Margaret Drummond as being of no consequence, as had Alex. How did they all know? A thought had been worming its way through my mind, ever since last night. It was Alex's remark about not having a drop of American blood in his veins. Since he claimed not to know his mother, how could he be sure of that?

Thinking this over, my eyes strayed to the pile of documents on my desk. My own work, shelved because of the events of the past few days. It might be better if I occupied myself with that and let the thought processes carry on in my subconscious. Sometimes they worked better that way.

I immediately abandoned that idea when I came across the request from a local family to check on antecedents possibly to be found in parish records in Forfar. I checked my map and found that it wouldn't take long to drive from Forfar to Banchory.

I set off at once. I made good time to Forfar. I had a few qualms about visiting Fergus McLachlan when I wasn't a Falkin. Strictly speaking it was none of my business.

I decided to play the innocent and say I had been on business in the area (almost true) and was just calling to apologise for not passing Mr McLachlan's message to Steven Falkin in time for him to make the trip, but to assure him Steven and Alex would be calling on him soon.

7

Skirl House was a tribute to Georgian architecture. It had all the correct proportions and grace even down to the columned portico where I sheltered from a sudden shower of rain, reluctant to make my presence known.

However, someone had clearly heard my car as I approached and within seconds the front door was opened by a homely looking woman with a welcoming smile on her face.

I hastily introduced myself and said I'd come from Drumbroar to make an apology to Mr McLachlan. I was ushered into a magnificent hall dominated by a wide staircase leading up to a first floor gallery. I waited on the chequerboard tiled floor and gazed around admiringly but quite without envy. Skirl House did not, after all, have the ancient character of Gilliestoun.

A few moments later a gentleman emerged from a room leading off the hall, introducing himself as Fergus McLachlan. He was a large man, casually dressed in moleskin trousers and a wool sweater. He was handsome with that rounded contented look that suggests good food, fine wine and a nature to match. A silky haired retriever padded politely behind him.

'Good afternoon,' I said, shaking his hand. 'I'm Lizanne Naismith, the person who took your call to the Falkin family the other day. I've called to apologise for unforgivably forgetting to pass on your message to Steven Falkin until this morning,' I paused to draw breath. 'Unfortunately by then he had already made arrangements to fly to Rotterdam.'

'Ah, he is going to visit the Broq company,' Fergus McLachlan smiled at me.

I was surprised that he knew that about Falkin Freight's business.

'It has been rather a fraught time in

Drumbroar,' I said, then tripped out a little lie. 'Mr Alex Falkin was also not available today so I decided to make amends.'

'You've driven all the way from Drumbroar just to apologise?' he said with concern.

'I had to be in Forfar today on my own business and realised Skirl House wasn't too far away,' I told him.

'Dear, dear, what a tedious journey for you. Perhaps you'd be good enough to stay for a while and have some tea with me, Miss Naismith?' he asked.

I felt a shiver of guilt that I might have tricked my way into his house and was about to decline his invitation when he said, 'I would like to ask you about Jeffrey's funeral. I'm so sorry I wasn't there to say goodbye to him. We were such old friends.'

Again I was surprised. I'd never heard anyone in the Falkin family speak of Mr McLachlan. Even Steven had not heard of him.

He ushered me into the room where

he'd evidently been working. It was an office-cum-library, the walls lined with books contrasting with an up to the minute computer placed in the centre of an elegant desk. A small fire burned merrily in the grate, a welcome sight after the gloom of dampness outdoors.

While waiting for tea, I told him about the service for Jeffrey and how much he would be missed in the community.

'We knew each other almost from the cradle,' he said after a moment's reflection. 'Jeffrey was the son of my father's steward and was brought up on the estate here. After his parents died he and Sarah went to live with an aunt in Drumbroar. We never lost touch, I'm glad to say. If he was in the area he'd drop in for a chat and a dram.'

The housekeeper brought in a tray then and she poured us tea. The tantalising aroma of home-baked fruit cake tempted my taste buds, but I hadn't the willpower to refuse the hospitality.

'I never visited Jeffrey in Drumbroar,' Fergus McLachlan went on. 'My father died when I was barely an adult and I was left to run the estate so I had little free time. Much the same applied to Jeffrey founding and running Falkin Freight, a fine company. He did so well and also in acquiring Gilliestoun Tower. Do you know it?'

'Yes, I have a museum in the grounds,' I said, 'but didn't volunteer any more concerning the Tower. I'm a friend of the family and they tolerate me there,' I tried for a lighter tone.

'Oh, of course, I forgot. You must have been there to take my telephone call,' he smiled at me.

Then he put down his cup and gazed at the fire for a moment. 'I never thought when Jeffrey called here last week that it would be our last time together. He was so looking forward to meeting Alex at Aberdeen.'

'You knew about Alex then?' I ventured, concealing my surprise.

He nodded. 'Yes, Jeffrey told me

about him some years ago and I have kept the secret well. No need for that now.' He saw my puzzled look.

'Jeffrey had his reasons for keeping quiet about Alex all this time,' he explained. 'He didn't want to upset the family.'

'I'm afraid it did, when Alex suddenly turned up on the doorstep and no-one knew who he was,' I couldn't help myself say.

Fergus McLachlan shook his head. 'Jeffrey could not foresee that he would not be there.'

I was instantly contrite. 'I know, it was the most awful tragedy.'

'And of course there was the mother to consider,' he said quietly.

I felt as if a sliver of ice was sliding down my back. 'Alex's mother?' I asked.

Mr McLachlan nodded. 'Jeffrey didn't want to keep Alex away from Drumbroar, but he was afraid that the revelation about his mother would be distressing to some.'

He must have noticed my mouth hanging open. 'That was one secret Jeffrey never divulged to me. I have no idea who Alex's mother was,' he said gently.

'I see,' I managed to say, noticing his past tense.

'Still, Jeffrey was making amends to both sons,' he nodded with approval. 'My offer to buy Falkin Freight was accepted by him and he intended to leave the money to the boys.'

'But his will stated that they would inherit nothing if the business was sold,' I blurted out.

Fergus McLachlan stared at me. 'You mean they don't know? He hadn't told anyone about the sale?' He shook his head. 'I thought he would have discussed it with Steven beforehand, particularly with reference to the offer from Broq.'

I shook my head.

'Jeffrey made a new will right here, after signing away the company. My housekeeper and I witnessed both documents. He asked me to send them to my solicitor who would forward them to Peter Clark. I presume there hasn't been enough time for my solicitor to deal with them.' He got to his feet and went over to his desk and lifted a folder. 'Copies of both documents are enclosed. Can you see they get to Jeffrey's solicitor?'

* * *

Fortunately the rain had stopped by the time I was back on the road. I knew my concentration on driving was being affected by the thoughts whirling about in my mind, so not having the windscreen wipers distracting me was some relief.

On the one hand I felt I was returning to Drumbroar with great news for Steven and Alex. They would both be able to choose their own way in life with sound financial backing.

Fergus McLachlan said that Jeffrey

had decided to retire from the company, giving him more time with his family.

'Provided all parties agree, there should be no problem with the inheritance. After all, the change only affects the two sons,' he said. 'I presume Steven has gone to meet the Broq directors since they had made Jeffrey an offer too. He considered it, but in the end he wanted the business to remain in Scotland. He was afraid Broq might take the business to the continent and all his staff could find themselves out of work.'

'He always did take care of his company workers,' I said.

'Yes, he was a responsible employer,' Mr McLachlan agreed. 'And in his way a caring father too. He told me that last afternoon that he was taking Alex to Gilliestoun to meet the family and to tell both boys they were free of the company. He knew Steven was itching to devote his energies to something else — extreme sports?' he queried.

I nodded. 'His passion.'

'Jeffrey had supported Alex through many endeavours in the States, but he thought if the lad was left to manage his own finances under his guidance, he might settle down with one particular career,' he concluded.

It was some comfort that Jeffrey had shown himself to be compassionate and thoughtful in the end. We'd all been so critical of him just a few days ago.

As I headed for the M9 another of Mr McLachlan's comments surfaced from the recesses of my mind where it had been lurking, disturbing me. The revelation of whoever had been Alex's mother that could 'distress some'. Did that mean that it could possibly be this *Margaret Drummond* in Drumbroar after all? Yet Alex, Dad and Sarah had dismissed her claim and Alex was convinced his mother was dead. Could it be that the writer was a relative of Margaret Drummond and only after money?

Could the threatening note advising

Alex to leave Scotland be connected to the same writer? Yet there had been something about it which seemed amateurish, while the other letter had a feeling of authenticity about it. The handwriting was so distinctive for a start.

A jolt of memory so startled me that I had to take a slip road and stop the car. My hands were shaking, my mind in turmoil. I had recognised the handwriting — or rather where I'd seen it before. But it was so . . . bizarre.

The spiky, jerky style was exactly the same as the lettering over Christina Dunure's pig sties!

No, it was impossible. Christina could not be Alex's mother. I couldn't envisage Jeffrey and Christina being a twosome. Their personalities were poles apart.

I sat for a few more minutes, composing myself. The only thing I could think of doing was to show the letter to Christina. I rummaged in my bag. It was still there where I'd put it after Alex had left last night as I had intended checking the parish records for the specific name. I laid it on the passenger seat and joined the road again, this time heading straight for the Dunure property.

It was dusk when I arrived. After her husband died, Christina had moved to a small cottage in the grounds of the Dunure farm, leaving the big farmhouse to Todd and Julia.

Before knocking on her door I slipped round to look at the pig sties. Yes, the jagged style of her writing was there in marker pen on wooden boards above each sty. *Braveheart, Macduff, Wallace, Bruce.* The names had been there a long time, most of the sties were now occupied by sows.

I trampled over to her cottage and knocked on the door.

'Lizanne!' She was delighted to see me when she opened the door, which put me off a little.

After a few more warm words and an invitation to sit down, I decided to come straight to the point.

'This letter was sent to Alex,' I said, passing it over to her.

'Whatever is this?' she cried in her distinctive way the instant she recognised her writing style. Then she read the message and gasped.

She looked at me. 'I am Christina Margaret Drummond Dunure. But I didn't write this letter and I'm certainly not Alex's mother,' she stood up.

'So who wrote it?' I asked.

She didn't answer me at first, but instead picked up the telephone and dialled a number. 'There's only one person who knows my full name,' she said.

'Todd, get down here immediately,' she commanded when the phone was answered at the other end of the line.

A few minutes later Todd came swaggering into the living-room.

He looked bored and hadn't noticed me sitting by the inglenook. 'Whatever is the matter now, Mother?' he drawled. He hadn't even bothered to look at her, instead making for a small table that held a few decanters.

On the way he saw me and stopped in his tracks. I saw his body language tense at once.

'Lizanne! What an unexpected pleasure,' he said, trying for a friendly tone and sounding completely insincere. He really was a despicable creep.

Without a word Christina thrust the letter at him.

'My, my, someone stirring something up,' he only glanced at it.

'Someone who not only knows my full name, but also can forge my handwriting,' Christina said coldly. 'Don't bother to deny it, Todd, just tell us why you wrote it.'

Todd turned a sly smile in my direction. 'Get this from Alex, did you? Holding his hand now instead of his brother's?'

I stared him out.

He then turned his back on me. 'Jeffrey forgot he had a daughter. Julia should have had a much larger share of the inheritance. You know perfectly well, Mother, that we need money. It shouldn't be given to some Johnny-come-lately American upstart.'

'What did you think this letter would achieve?' Christina asked, shaking with anger.

'I intend it to challenge the will,' he said, his mouth now a grim line. 'Stir up some mud. It's been proved that Jeffrey is Alex's father, but there must be some dark secret about the mother, otherwise we would have been told. I want that investigated in the hope that we find some reason to deny him his share of the will,' he said.

'Does Julia know about this?' I asked.

Todd gave me a little sneer. 'Not yet, but she'll be glad enough to get a better share of the inheritance.'

'Even though an investigation might make her father look bad?' I asked.

Todd shrugged.

'You forged my name for your dirty scheming with no thought for Alex's feelings!' Christina was white with fury.

Todd couldn't have cared less. 'It didn't matter whose name I chose, it should be enough to stir things up.'

'You've really sunk as low as you can go,' his mother told him. 'Using me in this way.'

Todd glared at her. 'Do you want us to lose Dunure Farm . . . everything? You and your precious pigs would be on the dung heap too.'

That was emotional blackmail, but two could play at that game. 'You only wrote this letter because your first one failed,' I said.

He stared at me. 'What first letter?'

I saw puzzlement, then a shadow of fear on his face.

'You mean there's another claim?' his voice was now a whisper.

I knew then that he hadn't written the threatening note, but I wasn't going to give away anything.

'Peter Clark has quite a lot to sort out,' I said enigmatically.

★ ★ ★

Weary though I was, I deliberately drove to the museum just to see if Steven's car was in the Gilliestoun driveway. It was.

I went into my beloved barn and rang Gilliestoun. Fortunately Steven answered.

'Can you come to the barn? I need to talk to you,' I said.

He grunted a reply, but I knew he'd come.

'I'm not long home from Rotterdam, I've had a bad day, now what is it?' he asked as he strode in.

I didn't pay much attention to his words, he was here with me and he certainly wouldn't have come if he hadn't wanted to see me, to talk to me. I decided to let him get it off his chest.

'How bad?'

'Dad had been approached by Broq who want to buy the company,' he said. 'Can you believe that he didn't even tell me!' He thumped one fist into the other palm. 'And they didn't believe me when I told them the terms of his will.'

He strode around the museum for a

while letting off steam while describing the way he'd been treated by Broq.

'You know, Lizanne, I'd sell it to them in a flash, if I could. Get shot of the whole caboodle.'

He came back to my desk. 'You seem completely uninterested,' he said coldly.

'I went, by myself, to see Fergus McLachlan today.' I held up my hand as I saw his face darken again. 'OK, maybe I was out of line, but it was my fault that you didn't get his message and I felt I had to apologise.'

He pulled out a chair and sat down opposite me. 'And so?'

As succinctly as I could I relayed some of the conversation I'd had with the man in Skirl House. I did not mention Alex, nor Jeffrey's new will. That had to go straight to Peter Clark first as Fergus McLachlan had insisted.

'Dad sold our company to this McLachlan?' he was astounded. 'Who is the man? I've never heard of him.'

'He is a long-standing friend of your father's. The deal was completed just a few hours before he died in the car crash.'

'But he never even breathed a whisper that he planned to sell,' Steven looked completely confused. 'How could he keep that from me?'

'According to Mr McLachlan he wanted it to be a surprise for you,' I said. 'All the details will be with Peter Clark in a day or so. I should think it will alter the terms of his will.' That was as far as I felt I could go.

'A surprise? A sop for discovering I had a brother more like,' Steven was cynical and ignored my point about the will.

I leant across the table to try to take his hand. 'Steven, you're going to have to accept that your father did things in the way he thought best,' I said, ignoring the fact that he snatched his hand away.

'Best for him,' he growled.

'Mr McLachlan says that the sale is legally binding,' I tried to comfort him.

He got the point. 'So my brother is

off the hook. No need to do even a day's work for Falkin Freight!' he drummed his fingers on the table.

'Maybe as compensation for never being acknowledged as part of the family, or the company,' I reminded him tartly.

Steven scowled at me. In that moment I knew my idea had all gone wrong. I had hoped that asking him to come to the barn and giving him the good news from Mr McLachlan might restore the closeness of our relationship. I probably sounded as if I was championing Alex over him. All I had done, it seemed, was to make the divide even wider.

I suppose my own sense of fairness had a lot to do with it and I opened my mouth to tell him about the letters Alex had received.

But I was too late. Steven got to his feet.

'No doubt you just can't wait to tell my brother about this new development,' he snapped. 'Well, I hope you're successful. I tried earlier to contact him, thinking I was doing the right thing, but he's left the hotel and no-one knows where he's gone. In other words, Lizanne, Alex Falkin has disappeared.'

8

My blood ran cold as Steven stormed out of the barn. Was this the end result of the threatening note? Had someone actually scared Alex out of Scotland or had he gone of his own free will?

When I arrived home, Dad's lights were out and it was then I realised how late it was. I let myself into my flat and slumped on the sofa. I had no idea where to begin to look for Alex.

My brain was sluggish after the long day but eventually reason prevailed. I claimed to be an investigator. Apply logic! Todd's letter had proved to be a false trail and since no-one had followed up the first letter maybe it had been false too? I remembered that I still had it somewhere and rooted it out eventually. It was certainly far more amateurish than Todd's.

Next I rang the Drumbroar Hotel

where Alex had been staying. The receptionist told me that Mr Falkin had paid his bill and left with his luggage, but without leaving a forwarding address. At least that reassured me that he hadn't been forced out of town.

I went into my kitchen to fetch some chilled water. It was then I saw the note on my worktop. It was from Dad.

Alex called in at the office today to go over papers relating to renting Semple Cottage. He wanted you to know. He was moving in this afternoon.

My heart returned to normal. I'd forgotten that he'd asked me to find out about some place to stay. My relief was compounded with a sense of comfort that he was keeping me informed of his whereabouts. Although all Steven's hints about me preferring Alex to him were completely unfounded I still felt a tenuous bond to Alex which I couldn't explain.

The news from Fergus McLachlan could wait until tomorrow. If I didn't get to bed now I'd be a wreck in the morning.

I had planned on opening my museum again that morning, but I felt it was more important to give Alex the news. On my way out I called into Peter Clark's office, gave him the folder I'd brought from Skirl House and told him about my visit.

Peter took it with an expression of relief. 'This morning I received notification of the sale, plus Jeffrey's new will and had no idea what was going on.'

I told him I was on my way to tell Alex, but that Steven already knew about the sale of the company.

I took my bike. Semple Cottage was situated on the far side of Loch Broar and I wasn't surprised it had been available for immediate occupancy. Not only was it something of an eccentricity, it was isolated and a long walk from town. Despite my dismissal of the threatening letter the previous evening, I was uneasy about Alex being in such a lonely place.

He was out in front of the cottage when I arrived, setting up a camera on a tripod. I parked my bike against the wall.

'My first caller,' he said cheerfully.

I went over and looked through the viewfinder of the camera. It was trained on the loch and in particular a nest on a small island in the centre. A swan's nest, no less. An ideal subject.

'I begin to see why you chose to come here,' I turned to face him.

'The opportunities for photography are great, especially for an amateur like me. Please come in.' He gestured to me to enter the cottage.

Semple Cottage had been built many years ago by a successful businessman as a weekend retreat. I couldn't imagine which architect, if any, had been consulted. The exterior was meant to represent a miniature Dutch barn which was odd given the situation in a loch-side wood.

'Come and see this,' he led me down a short passage to the rear of the cottage.

Once there he showed me into a small square room, completely bare.

'Isn't this something?' he sounded enthusiastic.

'A small, square room,' I stated the obvious.

'Ideal for a darkroom, Lizanne. Think photography. I'm going for it, the whole thing. Once I've finished my day's stint at Falkin Freight, I'll be straight back here to do work I really enjoy.'

'Ah, it's all clear now,' I replied.

'Since I have a job now, I needed a place to stay and my luck was in with this.' He beamed at me.

'Well, actually you no longer have a job,' I said. 'What you do have, or will have, is money from the sale of Falkin Freight.'

He frowned in puzzlement. 'You lost me a sentence or so ago.'

Briefly I recounted my visit to Fergus McLachlan, leaving out the bit about Alex's mother. I'd tell him about Christina and the *Margaret Drummond* letter later.

'Wow! That sounds like some deal. You think this is legal?' Alex asked after a moment.

'Mr McLachlan says it is and Peter Clark has all the papers now,' I told him. 'I don't know the finer points of the law, of course, but I shouldn't think any of the other legatees will object. It won't affect any of those who hold shares in the company.'

Alex was silent for a long time. I managed to hold my tongue, although I wasn't good at silences, as I felt he had a lot to mull over.

'Well,' he said eventually. 'Good for Dad. You know, Lizanne, I will not squander this money as I did with all he gave me before. Since I don't have to work at Falkin Freight which frankly would have driven me insane, I can choose my own career.' He let a smile spread over his face.

'As a photographer?' I guessed.

'Got it in one.'

'By the way, I made a discovery,' I said after a bit. 'The letter from

Margaret Drummond was a fake.'

'I knew that, but did you find out who sent it?' 'Todd.'

I watched his jaw drop. 'Him! Why did he do that?'

'He was using his mother's name hoping to challenge the will.' I didn't mention the possible dark secret of Alex's mother. 'Todd seems to think that Julia has been short-changed financially,' I told him.

'You mean that she won't get anything from the sale of the company?'

'No, but she did inherit shares. Jeffrey probably assumed Todd would provide for Julia, but unfortunately he's run through practically all their assets,' I said.

'It wasn't until I was coming back from the north that I remembered where I'd seen the writing in the *Margaret Drummond* letter,' I said, trying to lighten his mood.

'Where was that?' he didn't sound particularly interested.

'You'll never believe this! Above

Christina's pig sties. It was a shock, I can tell you, but I knew at once she could never be your mother.'

'True enough,' he still sounded detached.

'But,' I hesitated for a moment, yet I had to carry on. This was a man who had no idea who his mother had been. 'Fergus McLachlan knew about you, Alex. Jeffrey and he had been friends for years,' I told him about their early years together. 'Your dad didn't give him your mother's name, but I got the feeling she might have been Scots.'

'Really? Let's just leave it, Lizanne,' he sounded oddly dismissive.

I was astounded. He'd specifically asked me to investigate and now he was telling me to leave it?

'Leave it? You asked me to find out about Margaret Drummond — and I did — and now that there could be some other information, you ask me to leave it!' My voice rose an octave.

'This is my business. Butt out!' he snapped.

I almost reeled with shock. What was the matter with the man?

'I've been trying to help you — from day one in fact — no-one else did and now I'm cast aside.' I was boiling with anger.

'Sorry, Lizanne, that was rude of me. But really, I'd like you to drop it. I know my mother's name.'

'You what?' I whispered.

'Yes, I do. I didn't think you'd get so involved. I should have told you before that I'd . . . discovered it.'

'Have you known all along or just recently?' I asked, barely controlling my resurfaced anger.

He looked uncomfortable. 'No, I didn't know until . . . recently.'

'And I am not to know?'

'It's difficult.'

'After thirty years you find out who your mother is and it is difficult?' I could hardly contain my sarcasm.

'Since I discovered who she was I've been wrestling with the problem of whom, or if anyone, I should tell.' He

151

looked at me for a long moment. 'It's made me understand more things about Dad and why he acted the way he did. You've been a great friend to me since I came here, my only friend and above all I owe it to you . . . ' his voice trailed away.

I said nothing. I naturally wanted to know but in my heart knew it had to be his decision.

He finally made it. 'There's only one way to do this,' he said and reached into his back pocket for his wallet. From it he extracted a small photograph. 'I'm pretty certain this lady is my mother.' He handed over the photograph without looking at me.

It was a head and shoulders shot of a lady wearing a floral top of some kind. Soft fair hair framed her delicate oval face, but it was her eyes that were arresting — or rather their expression. She was looking straight at the person taking the photograph with an intensity that could only proclaim love.

I recognised her at once even though

the photograph had been taken before I was born. It was a picture of my mother, Anne, looking the image of Grandmother Elizabeth Anne's portrait.

'I can't believe you've done this to me,' was my first, instinctive reaction. I jerked my body into action. 'See you around, Falkin.'

Instantly Alex was on his feet, not exactly barring my way to the door, but certainly trying to stop me leaving.

'This was a huge shock to me, too,' he said, a gentle note in his voice. 'You see, Dad carried this photograph around with him all the time.'

I stopped then and turned to stare at him.

'I didn't know who the lady was,' he continued his explanation. 'Not until I saw the portrait of your grandmother at Gilliestoun on the day of the funeral,' he paused then finished with a tremor in his voice. 'When I asked about the portrait you said that your mother was the image of her. The photograph is of her, isn't it, your mother?'

I nodded and had to sit down again. My whole body was trembling now. At first it had been anger, now it was a whirl of emotional turmoil.

'Why . . . why didn't you ask Jeffrey about the photograph?' I managed to ask.

'He never knew I'd seen it.'

'How did you?' My questions were barely audible.

Alex sat in a chair facing me. 'I used to take money from his wallet when he came to see me. He never knew or if he guessed, he didn't say anything. I found the photograph one time, tucked away. I knew it was something private and to say I'd found it would be to confess to stealing.'

'Didn't you wonder who she was?' I was still shaken by the sight of the small photograph. Mother had been young, early twenties I reckoned, when it was taken.

'Of course, but when Dad showed me the photographs of all the family here I realised it wasn't his wife,

Evelyn,' he shrugged.

I said nothing, just kept staring at the photograph.

'When the police in Aberdeen gave me Dad's things,' he said, not looking at me, just carefully explaining the facts. 'I took the photograph from his wallet. I knew I would have to hand everything over to Evelyn and I didn't want the family to see it. And to be honest, I'd wondered on and off over the years if it was a picture of my mother.'

He was looking at it so fixedly in my hand that I passed it back to him.

'Can you think of any other reason why my father would carry a picture of your mother, secretly, for all those years?' he asked, after a moment.

'I suppose it does mean that she played some part in his life,' I said bleakly, hardly able to face the evidence.

'But you can't accept that she is my mother too?' his voice was sharp.

I was still trembling. 'You . . . you

didn't know my mother. She would never, ever, have abandoned a child.' My voice was shaking with passion.

'What if she had to? If there was a good reason,' he persisted.

'What good reason could there be for something as awful as that?' I cried.

'You once said to me that your grandfather had little time for my dad,' he reminded me. 'What if they were in love and he put a stop to any marriage?'

The whole idea was a nightmare. I wanted to weep.

'When did your father meet your mother?' Alex went off on another track. 'Was it more than thirty years ago?'

'I forget,' I muttered. I covered my eyes with my hands as if shutting out the whole scene. A hand touched my shoulder gently.

'Do you have a problem accepting me as a brother?' I heard him say.

I took my hands from my eyes and faced him. 'I haven't got that far yet,' I said. 'It's my mother — ' I broke down.

He waited.

'How could she have left a child in America to be brought up by someone else?' I wept. 'She was a caring person, our home was happy!'

Alex moved off then, running his hands through his hair. 'Honestly, Lizanne, I wasn't sure how to tell you, but I never thought it would upset you so much.'

'Do you realise that if this is true, then there were things about my mother that I never knew?' I blurted out, then caught myself. Alex had never had the opportunity to know her at all.

'I'll get some brandy,' he said and disappeared into the kitchen.

I was glad of the respite. I could see why Alex thought the photograph was proof. But Mother? Doing all this — and concealing it?

Alex returned with the brandy by which time I'd composed myself, at least outwardly. I owed him some consideration.

'Mother and Jeffrey — ' I began. 'I

157

can't remember precisely, but I never saw them pay much attention to each other.'

'Well, they wouldn't in public would they, if they had a secret?' he pointed out.

'I suppose not.' I sipped at the brandy.

'If Anne is my mother,' he said. 'It's possible that Dad didn't tell anyone about me because he was protecting her.'

'You mean that someone might have guessed?' I asked.

'I don't know, it just occurred to me,' he looked at me with hope.

'It's possible,' I conceded, forcing my mind to think over the suggestion. I wanted a comforting reason for what had happened.

'My dad adored Mother, I'm sure he thought he was the only one in her life,' I said. Again I sipped at the brandy, considering things.

'But after Mother died, why didn't Jeffrey bring you here then?' I questioned.

He shook his head. 'Maybe there was

still the possibility that someone might guess and that would hurt your father and you.'

Was that why Jeffrey had avoided me — and Dad too?

Alex went over to the windows and stared out. 'Could there be someone in Drumbroar who knew they were lovers?' he asked.

My head was beginning to clear. 'No, I would have heard something over the years. The town thrives on gossip,' I paused. 'There's only one person who might know.'

We looked at each other, having arrived at the same conclusion. 'Sarah,' we said in unison.

I told him then how tense she'd been the other morning when I was questioning her and the sudden relaxation when I mentioned the name Margaret Drummond as claiming to be his mother.

'She knew it was untrue,' Alex concluded.

'Mother and Sarah were friends,' I

remembered. 'They wrote to each other often.'

'We have to ask her if it's true,' Alex said.

'That won't be easy, she avoids me like anything. Was most upset when I turned up at Glasgow Airport with Steven, as if I was the last person she wanted to see.' Once again we stared at each other, enlightenment dawning. 'I've always wondered why she kept her distance like Jeffrey did.'

'Maybe they were both protecting you, in their way,' Alex gave me a rueful smile. 'I think that's why Dad never mentioned you or your father to me.'

'It looks as if it is all beginning to fit,' I heard myself say.

I stood up. 'I think I'd better go now. I'm still so confused.'

To my surprise he reached out and took my hand. 'I didn't intend to say anything to you just yet, Lizanne. I've had time to think about the situation. I didn't mean to throw it at you. I know it's been an awful shock.'

'Yes,' I admitted. 'It has. I need time,' I gently freed my hand.

He walked me to the door and I left, blindly heading for the lane.

Through the cloud of grief, another problem loomed. If this was true, how could I ever tell Dad that mother had had a child by Jeffrey? The knowledge would devastate him.

9

I went to my bolt hole — the museum. I had to be alone for a while to let the magnitude and emotional repercussions of my discovery assemble themselves in my brain. I shut the door behind me and automatically made myself some strong coffee.

It was at least an hour later before I realised the enormity of Alex's revelation was not going to take a measured length of time for me to assimilate let alone deal with. This was with me for the rest of my life.

I had loved and worshipped my mother. She had never failed me, never let me feel anything other than that she loved me wholeheartedly. If I asked, I would have described my childhood as warm and caring, allowing me to live a carefree life.

Sometimes Mother had been quiet,

usually pleading a headache, but it must have been heartache instead at the thought of the son she'd given up. She had carried that sorrow with her for years. How I wished I'd known, that I might have been able to comfort her. But then, for me to know, would mean that Dad would have known too.

Yet, Alex and I had finally met. I knew Mother would have been glad.

I was suddenly shaken out of my anguished thoughts by the ring of the telephone. It was the lawyer, Peter Clark. As a result of the sale of Falkin Freight an emergency meeting had been called and all the shareholders were asked to attend. He had already conveyed the contents of Jeffrey's new will to Steven and Alex.

I cycled back into town and on entering the Falkin Freight boardroom wasn't surprised to see Fergus McLachlan. He greeted me with warm courtesy.

I took a chair at the back of the room, deciding to distance myself from both Falkin brothers. Then it hit me.

One of those brothers was mine too! Evelyn sat with Julia and Steven. Sarah had a chair close by them while the other shareholders in the company were scattered about the room, Alex somewhere among them.

Peter Clark began by introducing Fergus McLachlan and producing the legal document that proved Jeffrey had sold the company to him. Mr McLachlan then took over the meeting. He promised all the shareholders that he had no plans to change the company in any way. Both Falkin sons had intimated that they no longer wished to hold any positions with the company, so he would take up the office of Managing Director, albeit in absentia, and the day-to-day business would be conducted by the present manager, Mr Maxwell, recommended by Mr Falkin, senior.

There were a few questions from shareholders, but no dissenters and the whole business was wrapped up in less than an hour.

Peter Clark had clearly conveyed to Julia some news. Alex had made a generous gift of money. I saw her warmly thanking Alex, her face transformed from its usual disgruntled expression to one of relief. Evidently the money would cannily be put in trust in her name, so Todd could not get his hands on it. Julia looked as if she welcomed the challenge of being in charge, but Peter Clark had also suggested that Christina help her manage the farm.

Sarah was with the group and I sidled over to be near them. If I didn't reach her now she could well leave for the States before I had another opportunity. Although Alex wanted to know the truth, I guessed he expected me to raise the subject with her. He saw me approach and nodded. He then neatly detained Sarah who had been about to leave with Julia, saying he'd like a chance to talk to her.

'Since I'm not planning to return to the States soon, perhaps I could take

165

you to lunch,' he said to her. 'Is it all right if I call you, Aunt Sarah?'

'Of course, Alex. It's time we got to know each other. I wish it had happened before, but well, it was difficult.' She shrugged.

'Time to remedy that. I know this cute little pub other side of the hill.' He took her arm. 'Lizanne is going to join us,' he said easily.

Sarah suddenly noticed me and once again her expression was wary. 'Of course.' She gave me a small smile.

Once settled in the pub and with our meal ordered, Sarah immediately opened the conversation.

'I was glad to hear that you're going to take up photography,' she said to Alex.

'Let's hope I make good.' He sighed. 'Going to college should be the right discipline for me, something missing from my make-up before. I always wanted to be a credit to Dad.'

'You had it hard. I didn't approve of what happened to you,' Sarah said, then bit her tongue.

Alex picked it up immediately. 'Well, that's all in the past now. I guess he valued your loyalty.'

Sarah shrugged. 'I suppose so. I didn't like it but I made a sworn promise to Jeffrey not to tell anyone about you.'

Alex let a beat go by and then said, very softly, 'And did you make that same promise to my mother?'

Sarah stiffened and I noticed anxiety cloud her eyes. She was unable to look at either of us, and clearly could not speak.

'To Anne?' he prompted with tenderness. When she didn't reply he took the photograph of our mother and laid it in front of Sarah.

'Dad always carried this in his wallet. I saw it one time when I was filching. He never knew I'd seen it,' he paused. 'I took it when I was given his belongings after the accident. I always wondered if it was my mother, but didn't know until I came here.'

Sarah looked at him, then me. 'How

did you know then?'

'When he saw Grandmother's portrait at Gilliestoun. He saw the
resemblance immediately,' I explained.

Sarah shook her head sorrowfully.
'Oh, Alex, what a way for you to find
out,' she laid a hand on his arm then
turned to me. 'Did you know, Lizanne,
when you were questioning me the
other day?'

'No, I didn't. I was investigating the
Margaret Drummond letter. I expect
you know now that was Todd's doing,' I
said.

She nodded grimly.

'I didn't know about my mother until
Alex told me last night,' I said.

Sarah's eyes were luminous with compassion for me. She clearly understood
how much it must have devastated me.

'You both deserve explanations,' she
paused, as if marshalling her thoughts.
'Jeffrey and I lived on the McLachan
estate for several years until our parents
were killed in a train crash, Then we
came here, to Drumbroar, to live with

an aunt. She was great and brought us up, but there was little money. We both left school with few qualifications. I got a job at riding stables, Jeffrey drove lorries.'

Our drinks arrived and we were all grateful for the distraction and sat for a moment, drinking.

'Jeffrey worked all hours until he had enough to put down a deposit on a lorry of his own. Falkin Freight was born, courtesy of the local bank. He drove himself to build up the company and it became the main employer in Drumbroar. He was very proud of that,' Sarah said. 'I had met Anne at the tennis club and we became friends and of course, through me, she met Jeffrey. It wasn't long before they fell in love.' She looked at me briefly. 'This was long before Hamish came to work here.'

'But they did plan to marry?' I had to ask.

'Oh yes,' Sarah said at once. 'But your grandfather wouldn't hear of it. he said he'd ruin Jeffrey if he didn't leave

Anne alone. Your grandfather was the local laird. In times past he would have controlled the whole town. As it was he had the power to discredit Jeffrey through his business contacts.'

'But that was awful!' I cried.

'Your grandfather was an aristocrat from a family line going back centuries. In his eyes a self-made man with no background wasn't good enough for a Lindsay daughter. That was the way society worked here then. The other factor was Gilliestoun. There was no money left to maintain it and your grandfather was looking for a rich son-in-law. Jeffrey was still developing Falkin Freight at that time.'

I was so appalled at my family's treatment of Jeffrey that I could say nothing.

Sarah turned to Alex. 'And then Anne fell pregnant with you. They didn't tell anyone. I was married to Howard by then and we had set up home in Arizona to breed horses. Anne came to the states to spend a few months with me — that was the story her parents were told. Jeffrey was coming to join her when the baby was due.'

Sarah twirled her glass round, deep in thought.

'Just before her due date, we had a message from Gilliestoun. Anne's mother had suffered a stroke. It wasn't fatal, but very disabling.'

'Mother would have been devastated,' I murmured.

'Exactly,' Sarah said. 'And to be honest, I don't think she and Jeffrey had really planned what would happen after the baby was born. But now Anne saw it as her duty to return home and take care of her mother.' Sarah caught Alex's disbelieving look. 'This was thirty years ago, Alex. That was how families operated then. And she knew that to bring home'an illegitimate child would probably kill her mother in her weakened state.'

'But what about my dad?' Alex asked.

'He was devastated. He knew if they

returned to Drumbroar with the baby your grandfather, because he was yours too, would try to take away everything he'd worked for in the town,' Sarah shook her head.

'And when I was born?' Alex asked, his voice taut.

'Before you were born they devised a plan to leave you in the States, try to sort out things back home and then come back for you. I couldn't look after you as I was about to have my first baby. I suggested cousins who'd emigrated to Tuscon some years ago and who were childless.'

'They never came back for me.' Alex was trying to hide his bitterness.

'No,' Sarah said softly. 'Sadly, when they returned to Scotland, Anne had to devote all her time to looking after her mother until she died two years later. So much time had passed that they felt it would be wrong to take you away, at that vulnerable age, from the couple who loved you as their son and they knew you were happy with them.

Sarah turned to me. 'I reckon the pain of parting with Alex was too much for them and they rarely saw each other. Some time later Jeffrey married Evelyn and then Hamish came to Drumbroar and met your mother. He wasn't the rich or titled man your grandfather had hoped for, but I don't think he cared any more, especially since Jeffrey had bought Gilliestoun.'

'You know,' Alex said reflectively. 'My adoptive parents gave me all their love and I would never have worried about not being theirs if Dad hadn't come along.'

'At the time I thought it was unforgivable of him to get in touch with you,' Sarah said, a thread of anger in her tone. 'He and Anne had made a pact to leave you alone, but he couldn't.'

'Did Jeffrey tell Mother about Alex each time he saw him?' I asked.

Sarah nodded. 'He wrote letters to her from my home thinking she'd want to hear. But Anne never forgave herself

173

for not going back for you, Alex. There she was, barely managing to cope with leaving a son six thousand miles away, but to hear snippets about his life broke her up. I used to get the most tragic letters from her.'

'So that's why she sometimes seemed remote,' I said.

'I suppose Jeffrey couldn't help himself,' Sarah said. 'He adored you, Alex, never stopped talking about you when he was with me.'

Alex merely shrugged.

'Jeffrey was fond of you too, Lizanne.' She turned to me anxious, I suspected, that I would understand her brother too. 'He admired your feisty attitude to Gilliestoun. When he eventually bought the Tower he insisted that the barn remain in Anne's possession, knowing you would inherit it.'

Was that why? Wasn't it because we both loved Anne — a love he could not acknowledge to me? 'I wish we could have been better friends,' I said and my response pleased her.

'You and Alex have both been hurt badly,' Sarah said. 'But now at least you have each other.'

Together we looked down at this little lady who had been given the enormous burden of carrying our parents' secret and also having to explain it to us. Alex took Sarah back to Gilliestoun but I elected to go home. They were adamant that no-one else should know our secret, but I pleaded that Steven should be told.

I was also still concerned about the first anonymous note Alex had received. It didn't seem to make sense. Who could want rid of him?

'Some crank wanting attention,' Sarah said when I mentioned it.

'I agree,' Alex now dismissed it. 'Throw it away, Lizanne.'

Once home I put the note on my kitchen table. Someone had written it, someone with a purpose, but what? It bothered me. I like solutions.

I made myself a sandwich when Dad arrived at my door. I offered him a cup of tea and he sat down at the table. I forced my mind away from Mother's story and tried to adopt a light tone.

'Once again Jeffrey surprised us,' I began. 'Imagine selling the company for the good of his sons.'

There was no reply and I turned round from filling the kettle to find Dad staring at Alex's note.

'Oh, just ignore that, Dad, some crank trying to upset Alex. He isn't going to go away, not now. And he knows all he needs to about his heritage.'

'All?' Dad asked in a flat tone. 'He knows everything?'

I slid into the chair opposite him. He raised his head and I saw pain in his eyes and set of his mouth.

'I wrote that note to Alex,' he said. 'I wanted him to leave Drumbroar.'

'Why?' I asked, then remembered his strange behaviour the last few days, as if he was trying to blank everything out.

'Was it because of his mother?' I asked, very gently.

He couldn't look at me. 'Sarah told you?' he asked. 'I thought she would know.'

'No, we actually brought it up with her,' I said. 'Alex guessed when he saw Grandmother's portrait at Gilliestoun on the day of the funeral. He had a photograph of Mother, taken from Jeffrey's wallet.'

'He only knew about his real mother from the portrait of another woman? You mean Jeffrey had never told him who she was?' He was appalled.

I shook my head.

'How . . . how did you know?' I asked then.

'When Alex first appeared I was amazed that Jeffrey had a son that no-one knew. Why keep it quiet since it had happened before his marriage to Evelyn? Why hadn't Jeffrey brought him here? These questions kept recurring in my mind,' he said in his precise way. 'Then it occurred to me that perhaps his mother was known to us, here in Drumbroar. I thought of other incidents that had puzzled me over the years. How Jeffrey had avoided your mother and me, passed me over as his lawyer years ago. Now I began to wonder if he'd had something to hide from me.'

He fiddled with his tea cup. 'I remembered your mother receiving letters from Sarah which seemed to upset her, although she didn't let me read them. I didn't know for sure, of course, but some things began to add up.'

I got up from my chair and went round to sit beside him, slipping my arm through his.

'It all happened before you came to Drumbroar,' I said.

He nodded. 'I know, and your mother and I had a happy marriage. Her sadness had nothing to do with me.'

He picked up the letter he'd sent to Alex. 'I wasn't certain of course if your mother had given birth to Alex, but I thought if he went away, you would never know.'

'You did it for me.' I was touched.

He nodded. 'It was a dreadful thing to do to Alex. I must see him and apologise.'

★ ★ ★

I made no real effort to reach Steven even though I was at the museum every day.

After a few days, Sarah left for her home, bidding me a tender farewell. 'I always wanted to be closer to you, Lizanne, but was terrified I'd let something slip,' she said. 'Promise to visit me soon.'

I promised and off she went to the airport in Steven's car.

He came into the museum on his return from the airport.

'I've decided what to do with my legacy,' he said without preamble. 'I'm investing in a sports centre in the Highlands. I'd like to introduce some extreme sports.'

'Something you've always wanted,' I said conversationally.

'I need time — need to get away from here and think about the future. Things have changed. Alex tells me he doesn't want to live at Giiliestoun, so Mother is going to stay on,' he was speaking more carefully now.

'I gather he plans to buy Semple Cottage,' I said.

'You would know all his plans, of course,' his voice was clipped.

'Yes I do.' I nodded. 'I gather Aunt Sarah said nothing to you.'

He frowned. 'About what?'

'Alex's mother.'

'She knows who she is?'

'Yes. And Alex does now.' I paused. 'I do too — and my dad. I'm going to tell you, but the knowledge goes no further.'

He sat down in the chair by my desk, his eyes never leaving mine.

'Alex is my half-brother, too. My mother gave birth to him in the States.'

Steven was speechless for a moment.

'Lizanne . . . you mean my dad and your mother? All those years ago? Oh

180

God, what a shock . . . especially for you.' He reached over and took my hand. 'Why did Alex not tell us before?'

'He didn't know until . . . well, Sarah confirmed it.' I didn't mention the portrait.

'How . . . how do you feel about this?' his voice was full of genuine concern for me.

'Once I got over the shock, regret that I never knew until now. I'm glad that he is my brother. That explains why I instinctively befriended him.'

Steven flushed. 'Of course. I misjudged the whole situation.'

I nodded. 'Anyway, maybe we need some time to think about the future.'

He looked at me for a long moment. 'You mean I didn't trust you.'

'Stuff happens.' I tried to shrug it off. 'Anyway, keep in touch, let me know how it goes.'

He got to his feet then, his expression bewildered. But he did need time — just as I did. Having said that, it was the hardest thing I'd ever done. I sent him away when I longed for him to stay, for him to say sorry, it had all been a mistake and he still loved me. But I didn't want him to say it then. He had to think about it. He had to be sure what he wanted for the future before it would have any meaning.

★   ★   ★

The weeks drifted into months. Alex was enthusiastic about his course and was taking pictures anywhere and everywhere.

To my delight he and Dad had become good friends after the awkwardness of the note was cleared up.

I had not even had as much as a postcard from Steven. Evelyn hadn't been slow to advise me that he was a very successful businessman now. She clearly thought he was out of my clutches.

I reflected that history had an odd way of repeating itself. The previous owner of Gilliestoun had refused to let his daughter marry a Falkin. Now Evelyn was glad that I no longer featured in Steven's life. In an odd way Gilliestoun had lost its domination of me. It was just an old house that had once belonged to my family. Life had to move on and I'd learned that people were far more important than stones and tapestries.

I knew the emptiness in my heart had nothing to do with the tower, but I had to tolerate that. That was until the day I had a phone call.

'Lizanne,' it was Steven's voice. 'I miss you. I need you.'

And my heart sang again.

Other titles in the
Linford Romance Library:

A HEART DIVIDED

Sheila Holroyd

Life is hard for Anne and her father under Cromwell's harsh rule, which has reduced them from wealth to poverty. When tragedy strikes it looks as if there is no one she can turn to for help. With one friend fearing for his life and another apparently lost to her, a man she hates sees her as a way of fulfilling all his ambitions. Will she have to surrender to him or lose everything?

SAFE HARBOUR

Cara Cooper

When Adam Hawthorne with his sharp suit and devastating looks drives into the town of Seaport, Cassandra knows he's dangerous. Not only do his plans threaten to ruin her successful harbourside restaurant, but also Adam stirs painful memories she'd rather forget. When Cassandra's sister Ellie turns up, in trouble as usual, Cassandra needs all her considerable strength to cope. But will discovering dark secrets from Adam's past change Cassandra's future? And will he be her saviour or her downfall?